The only person who can transform your life is the one you see every day in the mirror. Be you the one who shapes your own destiny.

Copyright

Timeless Stories of El Salvador Volume 1 by Federico Navarrete published by Supernova IC.

- federiconavarrete.com
- supernovaic.com

Every story is my personal adaptation of the oral traditions of El Salvador. Some narratives have an additional header, which highlights where I obtained significant inspiration such as blogs, books, newspapers, storytellers, videos, or websites.

No part of this publication may be reproduced, distributed, or transmitted in any form or by any means, including photocopying, recording, electronic or mechanical methods, or used for the training or development of artificial intelligence models, without the prior written permission of the publisher and author, except in the case of brief quotations embodied in critical reviews and certain other noncommercial uses permitted by copyright law. For permission requests, write to:

federicostories@protonmail.com

Cover and graphics created by Marcos Soriano.

Proofreading by Elizabeth Toole.

ISBN: 9798713597429

All rights reserved. Copyright © 2020 by Federico Navarrete.

Acknowledgments

Every story has a beginning, and this one is no different. It started in a tiny Central American country called El Salvador.

Throughout my childhood, adolescence, and adulthood, I heard, watched, and read countless stories. Especially while traveling to thirteen out of fourteen departments with my mom during the dry seasons—a time synonymous with spending the day eating tortillas with salt, accompanied by the elders, and reading my favorite childhood book, *Leyendas Cuentos y Adivinanzas de El Salvador* (Legends, Tales, and Riddles from El Salvador).

There are some specific individuals I would like to thank personally, starting with my grandfather Rigoberto Huezo. He encouraged me to read and always believed in me, even when everyone else saw me as a lost cause and only a future banana seller. He has been one of the greatest inspirations in my life, teaching me the value of education and encouraging me to pursue a Ph.D. one day and travel all over the world.

Going further, my grandmother Ofelia Zelayandia. Despite the distance and age, her love is immeasurable, and she always reminds me of a key truth during every call: "Everything is a matter of sacrifices." She shared with me unique religious legends and fairytales when I was a child and encouraged me to write a book one day.

Additionally, I would like to thank the greatest storytellers I have met in my entire life:

- Mr. Pablito (the security guard): He shared with me unique myths, mainly frightening and religious ones.

- Mr. Oscar (the bartender): He shared religious myths about how our societies have been shaped.
- Mr. Fidel (the chef). He focused on myths related to magical beasts.

These incredible men spent countless hours telling me thousands of stories every Friday, for around ten years, at the Lions Club of Santa Tecla.

Those nights at the club were indirectly made possible by my parents (Alberto and Marta de Navarrete). They took me to their social meetings, where I met these storytellers. They also gave me several books and shared more about our folklore, history, and culture, drawing from their unique experiences.

Next, I would like to especially thank my two brothers, Rodrigo Navarrete and Edgar Regalado. They have been by my side all my life, and most importantly, when no one else was, supporting and encouraging me in all my crazy adventures. Their support has been crucial to my success.

Additionally, there are four friends whose friendship has remained unchanged regardless of distance and time: Mario Argueta, Luisa Castellanos, Andreas Ellerbrock, and Darwin Bermudez. They served as my second pair of eyes as reviewers, and Mario put me in touch with Marcos, who created the amazing pictures.

Furthermore, there is one country and one organization I would like to thank for their indirect inspiration and support: Poland and the European Union. They supported my higher education, expanded my cultural intelligence and awareness, and helped me build a profession.

From Poland, I would like to thank one person in particular, Radosław Dąbrowski. Radek is my Polish best friend, the man who always listens to my crazy ideas.

Moreover, I am truly grateful to Mauricio Argueta from the Embassy of El Salvador in Berlin for helping me share my work globally.

Finally, there is one special woman I would like to thank: Eija-Irmeli Gnilka from Finland. She encouraged me to write this book, leave my comfort zone, become a writer, and bring the uniqueness of El Salvador to all of you.

Disclaimer

Most of this work is fiction. I adapted every story to an international audience using cultural intelligence.

In multiple stories, I provided some fictitious characters, dates, events, and locations as support to understand better the Salvadoran context. Any resemblance is purely coincidental.

This work is not a history book, and no one should consider it as one under any circumstances. Only a few stories represent real people, events, or dates in history.

Content

A brief history 1
Stories Map 2

Stories

The good and the bad Cadejo 4
The Siguanaba 16
Cipitio 22
The Headless Priest 26
The Black Knight 32
The Guirola Family 38
The Partideño 46
The Squeaky Wagon 50
The Owls 62
The Lady of the Rings 64
The Cuyancua 68
The Fair Judge of the Night 72
The Managuas 76
Chasca "The virgin of the water" 80
The Fleshless Woman 84
The Enchanted Ulupa Lagoon 88
Our Lady Saint Anne 92
The Midnight Yeller 96
The Lempa River 102
Devil's Door 106
Comizahual "The white woman" 112
Izalco Volcano 116
The Moon's Cave 122

The Amate Tree 126

The Pig Witch 128

The Tabudo 134

Mr. Money and Mrs. Fortune 138

Princess Naba and the Balsam Tree 146

The Tamales Woman of Cuzcachapa Lagoon 150

The Living Rock of Nahuizalco 154

Alegria Lagoon Siren 158

A brief history

BASED ON ENCYCLOPÆDIA BRITANNICA AND WIKIPEDIA.

El Salvador is a country located in Central America. It is the smallest and most densely populated of the seven Central American countries. The majority of its population is Christian. Its capital is San Salvador, and it borders Honduras to the northeast, Guatemala to the northwest, and the Pacific Ocean to the south.

Until the end of the 20th century, the country was primarily agricultural and heavily dependent on coffee exports. Afterwards, it began transitioning to the service sector.

For millennia, several Mesoamerican civilizations inhabited its region, mainly the Lenca, the Maya, and the Pipil people. Additionally, some archaeological monuments suggest an early Olmec presence around the first millennium BCE. At the beginning of the 16th century, the Spanish Empire conquered the Central American territory, incorporating it into the Viceroyalty of New Spain, governed from Mexico City.

In 1609, the Spaniards declared the area the Captaincy General of Guatemala, which included the territory that would later become El Salvador, until its independence from Spain in 1821.

Stories Map

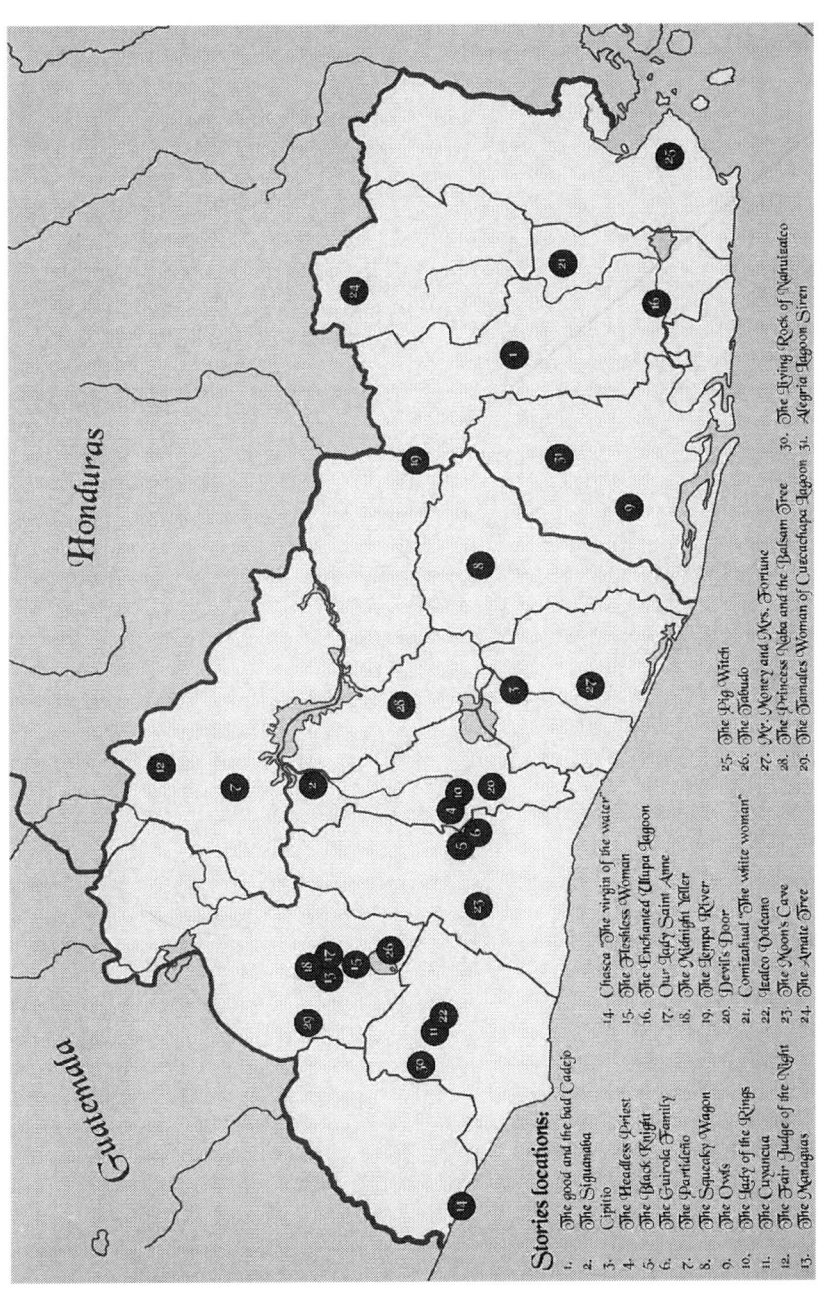

Stories locations:
1. The good and the bad Cadejo
2. The Siguanaba
3. Cipitio
4. The Headless Priest
5. The Black Knight
6. The Guirola Family
7. The Partideño
8. The Squeaky Wagon
9. The Owls
10. The Lady of the Rings
11. The Cuyancua
12. The Fair Judge of the Night
13. The Menguas
14. Chasca "The virgin of the water"
15. The Fleshless Woman
16. The Enchanted Olopa Lagoon
17. Our Lady Saint Anne
18. The Midnight Yeller
19. The Lempa River
20. Devil's Door
21. Comizahual "The white woman"
22. Ilcalco Volcano
23. The Moon's Cave
24. The Amate Tree
25. The Pig Witch
26. The Tabudo
27. Mr. Money and Mrs. Fortune
28. The Princess Naba and the Balsam Tree
29. The Tamales Woman of Cuezcachapa Lagoon
30. The Tying Rock of Nahuizalco
31. Alegria Lagoon Siren

The good and the bad Cadejo

Many years ago, I was coming back from the best party of my life. It was my eighteenth birthday, and I had finally become a man! That night was astonishing, and I had drunk Aguardiente for the first time! What a great night!

After the party was over, I was walking around my city trying to return to my home. I was not so sure about my path because I was blind drunk. However, one thing was crystal clear: this was an abnormal night. The sky was oddly clear, there were no stars, no moon, only darkness.

A few minutes later, I felt a strange, chilly wind. I had never felt anything like that in my life. I was trembling, when suddenly an unknown force made me turn around. At that moment, I saw two red eyes like embers in front of me! I heard a loud whistle, vreeew!

For a brief moment, I was blind with fear, but then everything became clearer and clearer, a massive being that looked like a black hound was in front of me. The beast was frightening because instead of paws, it had hooves, red eyes, and whistled eerily. I could not believe what was in front of my eyes! How was this possible? Was it the Cadejo? I thought it was just a legend for scaring children.

I ran as I had never before in my life until I reached my house, which was in the canton Loma Alta in Usulután. When I reached the door, I knocked frantically, unable to find my keys, and I could hear the same whistle behind me. The Cadejo was drawing nearer and nearer, and nobody opened the door. Suddenly, I felt the chilly wind again and saw the red eyes before I fainted in front of my house.

The next thing I knew; I awoke in my bed with my grandma rocking in her chair. She just asked: "Chepe, you met the Cadejo yesterday last night, didn't you?"

"How did she know? Was she a fortune teller?" I thought. We shared a cup of black coffee and had a long talk about my incident with the Cadejo and my wayward life, full of parties, drawing graffiti on the walls after school, and playing with girls' feelings every weekend. My neighbors defined me as the troublemaker of the canton.

After our talk, she looked at me very seriously and said:

"I see. Well, it is about time that you know more about our past. Also, to discover who the Cadejo really is, and most importantly, who its white twin is.

You can be sure, Chepe, this is a frightening story, but it is the right time for you to take responsibility for your life and understand what these spirits are."

It was the year 400 BCE when the first inhabitants of Quelepa, a settlement of the Lenca people, moved to a new land, a beautiful place, relatively close to a volcano. It was also next to an impressive freshwater river. In this settlement, a couple had a difficult birth of fraternal twins, the first in centuries. The town rejoiced in the birth of the twins. There were massive celebrations, and even the shaman and chieftain came to bless the newborns.

Several years passed, and these twins grew up. One had beautiful blonde hair, yellow eyes, and pale skin, while his brother had darker skin, black eyes, and curly dark brown hair.

The younger brother was called, "the Blonde" because of his lighter skin and calm voice. His brother was known as "the Black." He was extremely proud of being the black one. He was arrogant, strong, highly intelligent, fast, and extremely skillful in everything he attempted. The Blonde was calmer and submissive. He tended to follow his elder brother in all his mischiefs.

The town respected these twins because of their knowledge and skills. Most people praised them, and their family was extremely proud of them. Nobody suspected that one of them could be the wicked Cadejo, the creature that was terrifying the farmers every night.

The Black loved to frighten his neighbors because they were very religious. They constantly prayed to their gods because they were afraid of El Niño or La Niña, two climatic phenomena, which had murdered thousands of people in the past. These phenomena were the main reason why they relocated to Quelepa.

Every night he wore a costume made from eucalyptus leaves, which were painted with ashes and looked like a massive black hound. Then he hid in the scrubland of the mountains near the town.

In those days, people tended to go at night to collect sugarcane, cocoa, and other herbs because the weather was cooler. Like a mischievous boy, the Black waited for each townsman who passed by, and at that moment, he jumped. He pretended to be a spirit from the beyond who had come back to Earth to kidnap people and take them to the underworld.

While the Black was putting on this performance, his brother hid nearby, whistling to frighten people even more. His elder brother had dominated his soul and the Blonde was afraid of failing him. Even though he was against the idea of frightening his neighbors, he kept whistling every night, helping his brother.

The Black laughed every night and said, "Ha ha ha ha, what a bunch of ignorant people. If they knew I was the Cadejo, they would realize that spirits do not exist." He felt powerful and realized that because of his knowledge and skills, he was the Black, the only and real Cadejo.

The town started to believe that some spirits were coming from the Chaparrastique Volcano. Everyone was afraid to go there at night and investigate what was happening. However, it is common knowledge that no one should play with spirits because spirits are spirits, and common people must leave them in peace.

A couple of years later, his hometown and the nearest towns became really afraid of the volcano's black spirit. Nobody would go outside after 6 p.m., for fear of the spirit catching them. The Black became tempted to search for new towns close by.

One night, the Black and the Blonde were in a new town to frighten the inhabitants. Suddenly, the Black heard someone approaching and whispered to his brother, "Blonde, when I do this, you should start whist …" And at that moment, someone was next to them and said: "Good evening, boys."

"Good evening," the boys replied. They were perplexed because no one had noticed how he knew they were there. Or how had he arrived so fast?

"Could you tell us why you are walking around so late? Have I ever seen you before in our town?" asked the Black.

"No, I do not think so. I come from a faraway place," the old man replied. "I have been walking for a couple of days and might have gotten lost. I am just looking for some herbs for special work I need to do when I get back. What about you?"

"We were collecting some eucalyptus leaves for a potion for our sick grandma," lied the Blonde, who was shaking and very nervous.

"It seems you have collected quite a lot, have you not? I can see that your brother has a bundle of them," the old man replied.

"Kind of. We would like to get more," the Black lied, trying to sound casual.

At that moment, a lightning bolt struck a tree near them and split it in two. "Black! Let us go back home. It seems it is going to rain," the Blonde urged, his voice wavering.

"Do not be si—" before the Black finished his sentence, a strong thunderstorm had started.

"I saw a cave not far from here. Let us go and take shelter there for the night," said the old man.

They ran towards the cave, not pausing to consider the idea at all. They just wanted to get out of the rain.

As soon as they arrived, the old man instructed, "We need to collect some firewood for a campfire. I have some food in my bag. Can you gather some?"

The twins went out, and the Blonde whispered, "Black, did you notice something strange about this man?"

"What do you mean?" the Black grumbled, annoyed, as he hated collecting firewood at night, especially when it was wet.

"I do not remember this old man having a bag with him when we first met him," the Blonde remarked.

"Come on! Have you lost your mind? Of course, he did," the Black scoffed, sounding uninterested.

The twins could not gather enough firewood. However, when they returned to the cave, they found a huge campfire already burning.

"How did you build the fire so quickly? Where did you find the firewood?" the Black demanded.

"Well, you know, there was plenty of firewood right in front of the cave," replied the old man.

The Blonde started to shake. He did not remember any firewood, wood, or sticks in front of the cave. He whispered to his brother, "Brother, I do not recall seeing any firewood in front of the cave, do you?"

"Have you lost your mind? We just overlooked it," the Black snapped.

The Blonde was sure that something was not right in this place and especially with this man. The old man offered them cuajada cheese with tortillas and cups of corn coffee, which he claimed to have brought from his home.

While everyone was eating, the Blonde could not get rid of the idea that he had not seen any firewood or that bag. He glanced at the old man, then the fire, and then back at the man until the old man asked, "Am I handsome? Or what do you want? You do not stop glaring at me, and it is getting on my nerves!"

The Blonde was more frightened than before. He had thought the old man was only looking at the campfire, but somehow, he had noticed the Blonde looking at him.

"Has the cat got your tongue?" the old man taunted.

"After several attempts, the Blonde managed to say, 'I have a question. What were you doing there when we met you?'"

"I already told you I came here from a faraway place to collect some herbs to do a job," replied the old man.

"A job? What kind of work? You will not be able to find any special herbs here. We have only common herbs like chichipince or cat's claw, and they are everywhere," the Black responded, listening intently.

The old man smiled faintly. "You are quite the curious boys. Let me be honest with you. I work with what people feel but cannot see often. You can say, I am a shaman from the northern part of this land."

The Blonde's breathing quickened as a sudden realization struck him: he had not noticed the bag before, nor the firewood. "Black, we need to go back. We have to go back," he whispered, clutching his brother's arm.

The Black shoved his brother lightly, keeping his eyes on the old man. "So, are you a real shaman? You can do magic tricks, can't you?"

"Well, yes, I am a shaman, but you know, some things are best left unknown," the shaman replied, his gaze fixed on the campfire.

"What? What could be so secret that we cannot know? Spill it. You brought us here, so we deserve to know," the Black challenged, his arrogance evident.

The Blonde tried to convince his brother to leave. Something was not right at all, but the Black's pride had been hurt when the shaman refused to share more. They argued relentlessly, perhaps until midnight or later, before finally falling asleep.

The next day, the Black woke up with more energy and new ideas than he had ever felt before. At last, he could frighten not just the town, but the entire region! The old man had shown them how to truly transform into beasts at night, using a special potion made from rare herbs and a touch of unknown magic.

"The Black had not realized the shaman had left until his brother woke up and asked, 'Where is the shaman?'" "He must have left during the sunrise, but who cares Blonde! Now, I am going to be invincible! Ha ha ha!" answered the Black.

They walked back home, only to find their parents in a state of agitation. The twins had been missing for days or even weeks—no one knew for sure. Their mother asked them, "Where have you been?"

The Black partially told them the truth because he did not want anyone to know of his new powers, and his brother had a weak soul, so he only bowed his head and kept silent.

For days, the Black planned his new spectacle, knowing he no longer needed to hide in the bushes. Now, he would reveal himself at a special event in the city center, terrifying everyone like never before.

Everyone in their town was surprised that the Cadejo had stopped appearing for weeks. No one knew what had happened to it, but the town was happier as they had been since before the twins were born. Finally, the beast had vanished or moved to another place!

When the day of the event came, the Black transformed into a massive hound and was able to whistle like his brother used to do for him. In the midst of the celebration, he showed up and started to scare everyone. The frightened crowd ran around, trying to escape the huge beast. The Cadejo was back, but this time he looked more powerful than ever. He had new hooves on each leg, and his eyes were like red embers.

For countless hours, the townspeople remained terrified until the Blonde mustered the courage to drink the remainder of his brother's potion, transforming into a similar Cadejo. However, he was white and had blue eyes. He went to the city center and confronted his brother for the final showdown.

The Black did not know who the newcomer was. This was another Cadejo similar to him but in a different color. They looked at each other for a moment and began to fight and whistle for hours. Somehow, the Blonde managed to produce a louder whistle that only his twin could understand, saying, "Black, what is wrong with you? Let us end this once and for all."

"Are you nuts? Now I have everything that I always wanted," answered the Black. Hence their fight continued. After many hours, both of them were exhausted and tried to return to their house. The area was deserted. It was early morning—perhaps three or five a.m.—when they finally arrived. However, they were unable to enter their home. They knocked on the door, and their mom started to shout, "Devils! Devils! What are these beasts? We need hot peppers to ward off these devils! Olin, start a fire!"

The Black and the Blonde assumed the potion had worn off, as they no longer appeared as beasts to one another.

Their mother kept shouting, "They look like hounds, but they are not! Their paws are hooves, and they grow and shrink in the blink of an eye! Their eyes glow like embers, and instead of barking, they whistle as if from a distance—yet they are right in front of the house! Call the shaman!"

The entire town gathered at the twins' house, eager to find out what was happening. The crowd was stunned to see the beasts standing motionless in front of the house, only looking and whistling.

Both of them were frightened because they did not understand. Suddenly, the Black glimpsed a figure on the other side of the house—it was the shaman they had met a few nights earlier.

"Hey, boys, what is going on?" the shaman asked.

"Well, you know the potion should have expired. We followed your orders, but now, it seems that our parents cannot see or hear us," replied the Black.

"Really?" said the shaman.

"Wait! This was not a temporary transformation potion, as you claimed! You tricked us!" the Black shouted.

"Did your parents never tell you that curiosity killed the cat? I told you many times why I was here, but you forced me to reveal my secrets. Now you have your wish, and you are able to frighten as many people as you want forever! You look like what your parents said, a pair of hounds, which are not hounds, but have embers in their eyes," said the shaman.

"Please help us! Take this curse away!" the Blonde pleaded.

"Even if I wanted, my dear friend, I cannot. It was a choice you made. You were too feeble to face your brother before this happened. Plus, as I told both of you many times, there are some things we are better off not knowing, and you will never forget that you should not play with spirits," said the shaman.

"This is all your fault, Black!" yelled the Blonde. The Black just ignored him and complained, "You could have stopped me when you had the chance!" And they started to argue.

"Enough!" commanded the shaman. "From now on, every night, you will watch over all unfaithful men and women," he declared to the Black. He turned to the Blonde and said, "And you, you are going to prevent your brother from abusing others, protecting all good people."

"If either of you thought you could escape, think again. A powerful force will compel you to either frighten or protect those you encounter," the shaman warned.

After these last words, the shaman vanished in front of them, laughing one last time. They never saw him again, and only he knew the truth of their transformation. What could they do? They stayed like that and their parents, and their hometown who praised them never saw them again.

Nowadays, these two Cadejos are seen every night in the urban areas of El Salvador. Beware of your actions, for if you venture out alone, you might be their next prey!

The Siguanaba

INSPIRED BY VICTORIA DÍAZ DE MARROQUÍN'S VERSION FROM HER BOOK, LEYENDAS CUENTOS Y ADIVINANZAS DE EL SALVADOR.

Once upon a time, in a small Salvadoran village near the Lempa River, there lived a hard-working and kind Maya tribe. The tribe was recognized for always being helpful and peaceful. No one had ever been in conflict with them.

In this village lived a breathtakingly beautiful Maya girl who was admired by all the young men. Her name was Cihuehuet.

Cihuehuet's beauty was immeasurable. She had a fantastic smile, long black hair, penetrating hazel eyes, tanned skin, an hourglass figure, and was taller than average. However, nothing was more captivating than her beautiful breasts and her gorgeous face. Women from the neighboring villages envied her, and everyone described her as the most alluring woman of all tribes. Every village had heard of her, and many young warriors proposed to her all the time.

Without a doubt, Cihuehuet knew of her own beauty, and she had become so conceited that every time she went to hand-wash her clothes in the river, instead of hurrying up and doing her work, she stayed for hours looking at her face reflected in the clean and shiny waters of the Lempa River.

Several years passed, and she finally chose her future husband. She married the bravest and strongest warrior of all the Maya people, Tlaloc's son. Tlaloc was the God of rain, earthly fertility, and water.

Cihuehuet thought she had hit the jackpot because now, she was going to become part of a god's family, and she would have everything she had always wanted. Perhaps, she would become a princess! However, something unpredictable happened. A couple of months later, the shaman told her, "You are going to have a boy!"

Her life became a roller coaster between ups and mostly downs. She was shocked and scared because she knew once her son was born, she would have to stop doing everything she enjoyed. She would have to stop admiring her gorgeous face in the river or spending time with her friends because she would have to take care of her son! This made her miserable.

Nine months later, her son was born, and she looked for any excuse to leave her child alone because she was desperate to return to the river and look at her gorgeous face. Unfortunately, her husband could not take care of everything at home because someone needed to hunt and support their family.

A couple of years later, Cihuehuet got tired of looking for new excuses and just said, "My son is old enough to stay at home alone." She just left her house and went to the river without thinking twice.

One afternoon, her mother-in-law came to visit and was surprised to find the little boy crying at home, alone and eating ashes from the floor.

The old lady went out and found her daughter-in-law laughing and chatting with her friends by the river.

"Cihuehuet," she said angrily, "I have come from your house and found my little Cipitio eating ashes. Do not leave him alone! He is still very young."

Several months later, her mother-in-law came again, and one more time, she found the child abandoned eating ashes. At this point, she decided to speak to Tlaloc and ask for his advice.

She walked and walked for several days until she reached the source of the Lempa River in Guatemala. Tlaloc was wise and was already waiting for her. As soon as she arrived, he commanded in a strong voice:

> "Woman. Tell Cihuehuet that she is no longer single, and her life has changed forever. She is our grandchild's mother, and I command her

> *to take care of him! If anything else happens,
> you must notify me immediately."*

The old lady returned to Cihuehuet's home and told her Tlaloc's commands. Cihuehuet was furious, but scared so for a few months, she obeyed.

However, soon Cihuehuet "forgot" Tlaloc's commands, and when the old lady returned again, she just said, "Oh, my little boy! Once more, you are eating ashes! My Cipitio, you are getting really fat!"

The old lady returned and spoke to Tlaloc. He told her furiously:

> *"Enough! It is time to punish Cihuehuet! From today, Cihuehuet is going to become a horrible woman, who from this moment is going to be called Siguanaba. She is going to live on the banks of the rivers, handwashing her clothes forever. Therefore, she will see her ugly face reflected in the river all the time! Also, every night, she is going to frighten all wicked men for eternity."*

After he spoke these words, Cihuehuet felt a strange pain in her face. She was at the river and wanted to run to her house, but she could not. Her legs pulled her to the river. When she reached the river, a mysterious force made her see her new face in the water.

"Ouch! Who is this horrible woman?" she screamed, "Is it me? This cannot be! Haha haha!" She started to laugh maniacally. She had become insane.

From that day on, she vanished from the town, and no one ever saw her again.

Nowadays, anytime a man returns home alone and drunk, the Siguanaba appears in from of him as the most beautiful woman in the world. She is always naked or half-naked depending on her mood. She pretends to be humble and asks for a lift to her home.

After a couple of minutes or hours, the man always discovers that the beautiful woman is not a woman, but the Siguanaba! She suddenly transforms into her true form!

She starts laughing maniacally and stabbing him with her gigantic nails. If the man does not carry a rosary and starts praying with all his might, the Siguanaba pulls him to the nearest river, and no one ever sees him again.

Some survivors swear you can often see her near the rivers, Lempa, Torola, Toad, Jiboa, or Goascorán. They say they have seen her taking a shower with a gold huacal (a kind of water vessel) while combing her hair with a silver comb. Her magnificent body and exquisite breasts shine through her nightgown, and no man can resist approaching her.

The Siguanaba calls out to them and flirts until they rush to her. When they get close, she reveals her true, horrible face! They faint and do not remember anything else. They just know they met the Siguanaba because her curse forces her to live near rivers.

Other survivors claim that she hides behind the branches of Guaramo trees, as the elders say she was born from them.

Some of you might be wondering what happened to Cipitio. Is he still alive?

Cipitio is alive and remains a child forever. He lives with his grandparents, Tlaloc and the Siguanaba's mother-in-law, in Tlalocan (the afterlife). Sometimes, they allow him to visit nearby towns, where he throws flowers and small pebbles at beautiful girls handwashing clothes by the river. He does not intend to hurt anyone; he just wants to make them smile.

Some people also swear they have seen Cipitio eating ashes, but now he does it purely for pleasure, not out of hunger. If you ever meet him, do not be afraid. He is just another child, like you or I once were.

Cipitio

INSPIRED BY WAVES TOURS FIESTAS' VERSION.

Many moons ago, Cipitio was taken to Tlalocan, the afterlife, by his grandfather Tlaloc, the God of rain, earthly fertility, and water, where he would enjoy a better life by his side. Many people are shocked when they hear that a god brought an innocent child to live with him, away from his parents. However, Tlaloc was wise and had a good reason.

Everything happened one afternoon when Tlaloc cursed the Siguanaba, Cipitio's mother, and banished her due to her bad way of life. A few days later, Tlaloc called upon his son to tell him the bad news.

"Son, I have cursed your wife. She will live forever in the rivers, handwashing her clothes and frightening wicked men as punishment for her excessive vanity and recklessness as a mother. Also, I am taking my grandson to Tlalocan."

Tlaloc's son could not believe what he was hearing and replied, "Father, why are you taking all that I have? Haven't I worked hard enough to at least keep my child?"

Tlaloc answered, "Son, I understand, but you have more pressing responsibilities with this town. You will see your son again one day."

The man was furious and disappointed because his father took away everything he had: his wife, his child, his dignity, everything. They argued for hours until he accepted his destiny and left his child. He decided he would at least try to recover the love of his life. He started searching in every Salvadoran river, but he would never find her because he was a good man.

After many years, Cipitio was allowed to return to his homeland. Tlaloc blessed him and said, "My child, your time has come to visit your town again. You are not going to grow up anymore. You are going to be a child forever!"

Cipitio was extremely happy to return to his land. Perhaps, he would play with other children or meet his parents again. He had not changed a bit from his last time in El Salvador. He was still the same kind and chubby boy who loved eating ashes—a habit his grandmother had always tried to break while he lived in Tlalocan. However, nothing thrilled him more than wearing his new straw hat on every adventure.

Over the following years, Cipitio started to visit every river and town in El Salvador. At each stop by a river, he climbed on treetops; from there, he would throw flowers and small pebbles, complimenting any lonely girl handwashing her clothes. Many girls were flattered by this unknown admirer, while others felt annoyed.

Sometimes, Cipitio would follow certain girls, hoping they could become friends and play some games together. Sooner or later, these girls felt annoyed by his presence and went to their grandmothers, who would always recommend, "If you want to scare Cipitio away, you must eat your meal in front of a toilet bowl." So, they did, and he never showed up in their lives again.

However, you must remember Cipitio is just a child, like all of us were one day. He does not want to hurt anyone. He simply enjoys playing pranks and eating ashes from nearby villages.

Many villagers complain all the time because once in a while, they find a big mess at home, mostly near the kitchen. When this happens, they always yell, "Cipitio, I am going to catch you one day!" Nevertheless, only a few people know that Cipitio has his feet twisted backward, leaving his footsteps in the opposite direction while he walks through El Salvador. Therefore, if anyone tries to catch him, they will always walk in the wrong direction.

Other people say he can teleport from one place to another and laugh while he is doing it, but this is just a rumor. Cipitio indeed has some unique powers, but this is not one of them.

Anyway, if you ever want to meet him, you must simply have some Maquilishuat ashes with you during your lunch. Preferably in your kitchen, as Cipitio really loves them and feels more comfortable in that place. Perhaps, while you eat together, he will reveal to you some of his secrets (do not tell him that I told you this because generally, only children can see him). However, take care because he is a trickster and may play some nasty jokes on you, and the next day, you are going to have a mess at home.

The Headless Priest

It was a warm night during the wet season in San Pedro Perulapán in Cuscatlán. I was coming back home at midnight, dead drunk and exhausted after a great party on a Friday. I could barely remember where I was or which path I was taking. Suddenly, I collapsed on the pavement next to a church and slept like a log.

A couple of hours passed, and some bells started ringing very loudly. I woke up and looked around; I was inside a church that I did not recognize. It looked ancient, reminiscent of colonial times. I took my hat off and sat on the closest empty chair.

The priest was reciting in a language that I could not understand well. With some effort, I managed to make out a few words. My grandma always said that a hundred years ago, the churches celebrated their masses in Latin, but I was not sure if it was that mythical language, because I had never heard it before.

The church seemed empty, and I tried going closer to the altar because I could not see it. I felt the potent incense and the deep smoke. The roof was completely blackened from all the candles over the years. The faces of the saints on the walls appeared faded and opaque.

I stayed silent and followed the usual mass. Nevertheless, during the consecration, the priest looked forward to me, and something horrifying happened! A headless priest stood before me! My heart started to beat so fast that I almost had a heart attack! I ran to the door, but it was closed, and I could not open it. The headless priest approached me and tried to give me communion. However, at that moment, he vanished in front of my eyes!

I woke up in my room. I was sweating like a pig, and my wife was next to me; she was frightened because she said I had been yelling while I was sleeping and writhing in my bed.

I explained to her all that had happened the previous night. She glared at me and urged, "Rolando, you must visit Mr. Gilberto, Mrs. Rosario's nephew. He had a similar experience in the past."

Next Sunday, I rode my horse to Mr. Gilberto's cabin. He was a very old man who lived at the top of a mountain about 50km from our house in San Pedro Perulapán, but I was able to reach his house.

I was shocked because the house seemed abandoned as if no one had lived there for years. I felt some cold air behind me, I turned around, and the old man was in front of me. Mr. Gilberto asked me: "Who are you? What are you looking at in my house? Do I know you?"

I explained everything that had happened and mentioned that my wife had sent me to him. He simply replied, "I see. Come, we need to speak more in the basement."

Mr. Gilberto lit some candles and instructed, "Sit down. I will bring some coffee. Do not move."

After waiting for half an hour or more, he finally returned and asked, "Do you know what happened to you yesterday?"

I answered that I was not sure because I had never experienced something like that before, and I was still shaking when thinking about it.

"Rolando, something is not going well in your life. You must stop this life of sins and infidelity. Until you do that, the headless priest is going to chase you in your dreams," he said.

"Do you know why the headless priest appears or what happened to him?" asked Mr. Gilberto.

I honestly told Mr. Gilberto that I knew nothing about him. I had just overheard some stories about him from time to time, but I had never cared about him.

"So, it is about time that you got to know a little about our past," Mr. Gilberto remarked.

This is an old story dating back to the colonial period. The conquest was ongoing 200 years after the Spaniards were well-established in America. They started the forced conversion of our people. They brought Catholicism to our lands and many good and bad people too.

In those days, priests wielded incredible power. They influenced all spheres including politics, education, science, in fact, everything. Every new decision or law had to be approved by their council.

The Archdiocese assigned one of their most handsome and well-educated priests to a church known as Our Lady of Mercy *(Nuestra Señora de La Merced in Spanish)* in San Salvador. This priest's life was challenging because many women had tried to pervert him over the years. He overcame most of his temptations. However, one day, a woman confessed to him, and her beauty and sweet-voiced tormented him to such an extent that he could not stop thinking about her for many nights.

The priest requested a relocation, but the Archdiocese declined it. He was an important figure, and no one wanted to take his role. The priest did everything in his power to resist, but one day, he succumbed to his nature and committed a great sin. He had a romance with a young widowed woman.

This event sparked a series of secret encounters with her in remote areas on some weekends. For several months, he kept their meetings a closely guarded secret. No one suspected such a respected and loved member of society could be involved in these things.

However, one day, a man discovered his secret activities while he was visiting a remote village. Upon his return, he went from house to house, spreading the news throughout the city. This scandal tarnished his once-respected reputation, and he fled to the mountains, ceasing his encounters with the woman while continuing his priestly duties in secret.

He never confessed his sins and was mistakenly killed during a peasant revolt. He was beheaded, and his hands were full of sores.

After that, many people said that he came back to his old church to purge his sins until the end of time. Moreover, he seeks to help people like you, Rolando, to overcome their bad habits and put their lives back on the right path.

Many people say he tends to walk around midnight between the churches of The Rosary and Our Lady of Mercy in San Salvador. He follows a specific path. He starts at the Church of The Rosary, and later takes the 6th Avenue towards the former cinema Libertad. After that, he turns around the 6th eastern street, and finally, turns around the 6th northern street before he enters the Church of Our Lady of Mercy. Later, he vanishes. In the 1920s, several people claimed to have seen him wandering on the old La Vega bridge before disappearing before their eyes. One thing is common in all his apparitions; he wears his old black habit, a rosary, and a cross.

However, your case is very specific because it is when he turns up in his former church. This is dangerous because you saw him in the atrium walking around the bell tower. Be careful, Rolando, these habits are pretty bad. If you do not change your ways, I might never see you or your wife again.

Rolando, more shaken than he had ever been in his life, said, "Thank you, Mr. Gilberto. I must tell my wife everything, and I will stop seeing my lover. I need to go immediately!"

After Rolando left, and before the last candle blew out, Mr. Gilberto said in Latin, "Quam iste mihi reddant, si nobile. Spero me in somnis autem non ad terrent! Hahahahahahaha!"

That means:

"This man is cleverer than I thought, perhaps even noble. I hope I will not need to scare him again in his dreams! Haha haha!"

The Black Knight

It was a dark and cold night in the middle of 1911. I was riding my horse near the old Guirola estate in Santa Tecla. That night was foggier than I had expected; I could barely see what was in front of me. I had lost track of time, but then I heard the Church of Saint Anthony's clock ringing. It was midnight.

On my way back, I noticed a spectacular light at the top of a hill not far from Guirola's cottage when suddenly, a black rider reared his black horse at a great speed next to me. I would remember that moment for the rest of my life because I had met The Black Knight!

Several myths surrounded the Guirola Family due to their immense wealth and power, which, according to legend, had been granted by The Black Knight. They belonged to an elite group known as *The 14 Families.*

It was clear to me that I had to escape from that place. I spurred my horse to run faster than ever. We needed to reach home. We could not stay here any longer! All legends say, "if The Black Knight catches you, you will never see daylight again!"

I tried to force my horse to run faster, but it seemed something was stopping us. The soil looked different, and for every step forward, we seemed to move three steps backward. I was desperate, and I recalled there was an abandoned ranch not so far from here. We went there to spend the night.

The next morning, I had a terrible headache, and all my body hurt. My horse also seemed affected. We waited until midday to go back home.

When I arrived home, my wife was crying and shocked as if she had seen a ghost. She sobbed, "Last night, The Black Knight was seen and kidnapped one of Mr. Guirola's sons. He was known as a good and humble man. I do not understand why this happened, and you were not here! I was scared he might have taken you too." Suddenly, she hugged me as if there was no tomorrow.

Until that night, I was quite skeptical about this old legend. However, I wanted to know more about it, so I went to visit Mr. José, an old sergeant from the Salvadoran marine. He did not live far, just next to the San Salvador Volcano. Most people said he had lost his mind after many bar fights and battles, but I still thought he was a good man.

When I arrived, he was sharpening his machete in front of his house, and he immediately said, "Hey Juan! Long time no see. What brings you here?"

"Well, Mr. José, do you know what happened to Mr. Luis yesterday?" I asked him.

"If you mean Mr. Guirola's son, yes, Juan, I know. Unfortunately, his time came. It had been seven years since The Black Knight last visited them."

A shiver ran down Mr. José's spine, leaving him uneasy. He hesitated for a moment before continuing, "So, what about you? Did you meet him?"

"Honestly, yes, yesterday I saw him while he was in their house, and I ran away. Now, I would like to know more about him. Do you know anything?" I asked.

"Hmm," Mr. José thought for a moment. "Well, it is an old legend. They say he is the very beast from hell. Are you sure you want to know more?" he continued.

"I would rather prevent something like that from happening to me, please tell me," I replied.

"Okay, I will tell you what I know. Please take a seat," began Mr. José.

In all the rural areas like Santa Tecla, poverty had been rampant ever since the post-Columbian era. Many people suffered from different illnesses and problems. Some people wanted to become wealthier faster in our society. They were just jealous of the oligarchs' wealth, and they wanted a shortcut to become as powerful as them.

One night, one of these envious men was walking back to his humble home when an elegant man on a black horse approached him and asked, "It is quite late. Do you need a ride on my horse?"

The poor man answered, "Definitely, that would be very kind of you. I am exhausted after work."

On their way back, the elegant man spoke to him for a while, claiming to be a kind of magician who could grant him anything he desired: wealth, happiness, a beautiful wife—anything at all.

The man was suspicious of the offer and asked, "Why would you give me anything I want if you do not know my name? What is the trick behind it?"

"Indeed, I can give you everything you have dreamed of, Miguel, and even more, but there is a small condition. After seven years of prosperity, I will come back and take you with me to another place. If you agree, I will give you everything you desire," the elegant man replied.

Miguel was shocked because the elegant man knew his name, but he did not know his. Terrified and uncertain, he agreed to think about it.

The two men continued riding in silence. After a few moments, the elegant man said, "If you ever accept my offer, during the full moon, you must go to a secluded place, smoke a cigar, burn some chichipince incense, and say three times, 'Mr. Black, come and give me all that I want!'"

After those final words, the elegant man left Miguel at his home and vanished before his eyes, as if he had never existed. Only then did Miguel realize that they had already reached his house.

The following months were extremely tough. Miguel lost everything because of El Niño. A severe drought destroyed his small plantation and everything around El Salvador. Also, he lost his job and failed to find another. He was hungrier than he had ever been in his life.

Miguel became angry and desperate because he could not find a solution to all his problems. His debts skyrocketed, and poverty spread throughout the entire country. However, one night, he remembered The Black Knight's words. He pondered for a few days, but in the end, his desperation grew too strong to resist. He followed the elegant man's instructions, invoking him in a lonely place near a river during the blood moon, saying aloud three times, "Mr. Black, come and give me all that I want!"

The Black Knight appeared as he had promised and asked, "So Miguel, what do you want?"

Seven years later, all had changed in El Salvador, a Coffee Oligarchy had been born, and it was a prosperous time. Miguel's life was full of happiness, wealth, mansions, servants, a beautiful wife, and everything he had always dreamed of. He was part of the oligarchy, but he had forgotten that he had advocated The Black Knight seven years ago.

One night, an elegant man came to Miguel's estate and requested his presence. One of the servants went inside and informed Miguel about the visitor. Miguel turned pale and started trembling like a leaf. Instead of facing him, he ordered his servants to protect him and throw the man out. However, The Black Knight was the true devil, and he effortlessly broke through the servants, entered Miguel's estate, and took his soul—making Miguel the first documented victim.

During the following years, more and more people made deals with The Black Knight out of jealousy or because their lives had turned bad. Their dreams of wealth or ambitions to recover everything were more powerful than the fear of bargaining with their souls.

And as always, after they had invoked The Black Knight, he appeared in a black whirlwind as an elegant rider dressed in black riding his powerful steed, granting them everything they desired. The next morning, villagers nearby could always smell burning wood and sulfur. This unmistakable scent became a clear sign of his presence.

As you could guess, Juan, The Black Knight's real business is to exchange people's souls for wealth, power, women, happiness, everything you want in life. However, the curse is not only for the person who invoked him, far from it—it extends to the next seven generations, binding them to the deal and ensuring their misfortune continues.

"And that is all that I know, Juan," said Mr. José, concluding his story.

Juan was scared and only replied: "Thank you for sharing your valuable knowledge, Mr. José. From now on, I will be more careful every night when I return home late."

After Juan left, Mr. José muttered, "Hopefully, you will not be so careful!" Then, he vanished from his cabin, looking for new souls.

The Guirola Family

INSPIRED BY "LA EXTRAÑA LEYENDA DE UNA FAMILIA" AND "LA MANSIÓN GUIROLA Y "LA HISTORIA DE LA ENIGMÁTICA FAMILIA"" FROM EL DIARIO DE HOY BY MARVIN GALEAS AND NANCY HERNÁNDEZ RESPECTIVELY.

Long ago, in the early 1800s, a tall, white, and good-looking man appeared from nowhere on a cold night, along the cobbled streets of Zacatecoluca. He settled there and lived in a tiny cabin. He had a lonely and melancholic air and claimed to be Rafael María Guirola.

Mr. Rafael was born in Spain and became a successful businessman in El Salvador, where his first businesses were related to trading. He got married to Gertrudis de la Cotera y González, a woman of Spanish descent, and after their marriage in 1826, they had a son, Ángel Guirola de la Cotera.

Ángel was sent by his family to study for his bachelor's degree in Guatemala City. After his graduation, he worked for a couple of years in one of the largest pharmacies there, owned by Mr. Pío Porta.

In 1844, Ángel returned to El Salvador, where he spent all his savings and took out loans to purchase land, which he dedicated to indigo cultivation. He showed a great ability for exporting this product and extended his business throughout the Caribbean, Panama, and the United States of America.

Over the years, the Guirola family expanded their businesses from indigo to coffee and cotton. They were also among the first merchants to import accessories and fabrics from Europe. Their wide range of products was advertised in the Government Gazette *(El Diario Oficial in Spanish)* on January 1st, 1879, they advertised:

> *"In Mr. Ángel Guirola's house in Santa Tecla the following items are sold wholesale and retail: good and fine coffee; golden galleries, French and English material for curtains; tassels for said curtains; patent leather goods for folders and other uses; flat, white and colored glasses, doll models, painted metal sinks, envelopes, and groceries; Castilla wax in loaves of 1 and 25 pounds; olive oil in all sizes, castor and almond oil in small bottles, sweet and dry wines, champagne, fine and ordinary cognac, oil paints, zinc sheets, hoes, country*

> *imitation brakes, iron chains for mules and horses, revolvers, two-caliber shotguns, rifles and ammunition, tarpaulin covers for cars, white bibs for shirts, white nightgowns, and fat cattle."*

They without a doubt started multiple business revolutions in El Salvador. Many people believe they began the rise of the coffee business because it became their flagship export product and the source of most of their wealth.

Everything seemed picture-perfect until 1858 when something intriguing occurred: Ángel married a wealthy Jamaican woman named Cordelia Duke Alexander in New York.

The gossip was that she knew how to perform supernatural rituals from beyond, commonly practiced in her Caribbean region. Some of those rituals were about making deals with wicked spirits. Cordelia was the person who, according to the legend, encouraged Ángel to make his famous deal with the devil.

Rumors spread like wildfire around the country about his deal with the devil. Especially after some unusual guests started visiting their house at very late hours, like a gentleman dressed in black, riding a black horse. Their servants thought it was The Black Knight, and on those nights, everyone who lived in the surrounding area saw mysterious lights and heard inexplicable noises, which gave rise to many unrealistic stories.

According to legend, Ángel's deal with the devil was as follows:

> *"Ángel will get all the fortune and youth that he has dreamed for him and his family in exchange for his soul and the next seven*

generations. To retain their wealth, each new generation needs to sacrifice one child in the devil's name."

Many people suspected the origins of his fortune. It was believed that to become as wealthy as Ángel, one had to go to a secluded place at night, smoke a cigar, recite special prayers, burn specific incense, and summon The Black Knight. After he appeared, the person would make their deal.

Ángel had such incredible solid business acumen and possessed so many properties and investments around El Salvador that no one could explain how this had happened overnight. His employees, who frequently gave people alternative names, referred to Mr. Guirola as Mr. Virola. Until today, the Guirola family has a peculiar nickname in Zacatecoluca "the Viroleños."

The Guirola family relocated to Santa Tecla in 1866 and quickly became distinguished members of society because they owned practically everything: lighting, water, public transport, forest trees, and the animals that lived there. Additionally, subsequent generations of the Guirola family continued to profit from their significant wealth, eventually joining an exclusive group of feudal lords known as The 14 Families. These families ruled El Salvador for decades.

In the same year, they completed their splendid mansion in Santa Tecla. It evoked the Parisian residences. On its roof, they had two eagle statues erected, seeming to majestically guard the entire city. The residence was called The Eagles Mansion for this reason. The Guirola family organized exclusive parties in their mansion, where they consumed concoctions made from bats' blood mixed with fine European liqueurs.

Some of the people who attended their exclusive parties said that one of the family members had a room lined with silver coins, and on the roof of it, there was a symbol resembling a goat.

Others said the Guirola family sacrificed beautiful maidens from time to time. Many local beautiful women, regular visitors to the family home, claimed that the family subjected local women to various sexual practices, particularly the so-called "Comadres de Velorio," who visited the house after any death to attend the wakes. No one ever saw these women again.

One member of the Guirola family used to walk around Santa Tecla dressed entirely in black suits. He was accompanied on these walks by a dozen enormous black dogs. These dogs were unique because the family had ripped out their fangs and replaced them with new ones of pure gold.

The Guirola family had many properties, but their former cottage is considered one of the most splendid pieces of art in El Salvador. The architecture is Victorian, and each of its six rooms has a unique European style, including Italian, French, and Spanish.

However, people who live these days in the surroundings (in the El Paraíso neighborhood) believe it is a haunted place. They swear they have experienced paranormal events such as lights turning on and off without reason during their community meetings, and there is a mirror in one of the bathrooms that reflects an old lady sitting in a rocking chair waving from an unknown living room.

Some residents say, in the late 1980s, when the construction of the neighborhood was still in progress, some employees found a couple of unusual bags underground near the cottage. They called their boss (Mr. Campos) to inspect them. He came, picked them up, and never returned. Nobody knows what was inside those bags.

Incredibly, multiple stories keep surrounding this family even in the 2000s, despite the fact that their power and influence have significantly faded over the generations, especially after the Salvadoran Civil War. However, one particular event renewed public interest in this family one more time.

One of their last mansions located near the Las Colinas neighborhood surprisingly survived an earthquake in 2001 almost intact, when hundreds of houses next to it were buried because of a landslide. Many people believe that the mansion shifted from its original location. In the years that followed, visitors reported bizarre and unrealistic experiences.

Many youngsters claim that on the top floor, there is a cold room where a gigantic portrait of Mr. Guirola hangs. Some of them say they entered there, and when they looked at the picture, they fainted immediately afterward.

Other people say they met an uncommon pair of uniformed girls on Thursdays at 3 p.m., who asked to accompany them through the back door. Anyone who declined heard a strange proposal. The girls said that they would return every Thursday at the same time if they would like to join them.

On rare occasions, some people affirm, two unexpected and scary scarecrows appear close to the mansion.

Surprisingly not even their former cottage has escaped from new stories. Several months after the 2001 earthquake, some new inhabitants innocently shared with the community that they had seen some beautiful, enormous, and peaceful black dogs chained to some trees behind the cottage, and they wanted to know the owner.

The residents were puzzled because no one had lived there for years, and they did not know of any dogs living there. Only for a brief period, some security guards inhabited it, but they did not have any black dogs. Some people even tried to find these mysterious dogs, but they could not find any trace.

Several other strange incidents have occurred over the years that keep this story alive. Even today, a few old Salvadorans swear some family members never aged, but because of their deal, their life was full of tragedies. Unfortunately, many family members died in mysterious accidents that remain unexplained to this day, further reinforcing the legend of their deal.

Over the decades, many people have embellished the family's journey through popular stories. However, most of them came from classical literature such as Goethe's Faust, Dracula, Bluebeard, and The Picture of Dorian Gray.

The truth is that Ángel Guirola was a good and honorable man, a philanthropist, and one of few people to pioneer in agriculture. Furthermore, he was a deputy, vice-president of El Salvador, and briefly held the presidency during Dr. Rafael Zaldívar's administration in 1884.

Ángel was an untiring man, who after his career as a politician, continued running his businesses. In 1885, he founded a bank called Banco Particular de El Salvador in collaboration with J. Maurice Duke, Francisco Camacho,

Emeterio S. Ruano, JM Alexander, and others. In 1891, the bank was renamed Banco Salvadoreño.

Later, between March and June 1885, Ángel mediated during General Justo Rufino Barrios' invasion and the revolution led by General Francisco Menéndez. After General Menéndez's triumph, he traveled through the USA and Europe.

However, little by little, the Guirola family lost their economic and social power, mainly when coffee cultivation began to decline, and crises such as the Great Depression of 1929 hit El Salvador's economy badly. Nevertheless, their legacy endures to this day through the numerous significant properties they donated in Santa Tecla, such as,

- A beautiful natural park called El Cafetalón.
- A large property for a foster home, dedicated to the memory of Ángel's son, Adalberto, who died during the war with Guatemala in 1906. Ángel donated one hundred thousand Salvadoran pesos to establish it.
- A building for a hospital to care for the poor and needy called San Rafael.

The Partideño

Many years ago, an unusual man appeared from nowhere in the lands of Chalatenango. He possessed magical powers similar to the Pied Piper of Hamelin because whenever he walked next to an animal, they would follow him. He used his powers to amass a fortune by stealing the finest livestock from northern Chalatenango and southern Honduras. For unknown reasons, the locals called him the Partideño.

The Partideño was an unfriendly and grumpy character, who lived alone in a secret cave in the mountains near El Pital Hill, where no one could find him.

One day, a townsman was walking alone in those mountains when he saw the Partideño talking to a young man. The Partideño was telling the youngster that he had obtained his unique powers from a special deal with The Black Knight and that maybe the boy should consider a deal as well because he knew where to find the knight. The townsman was shocked and ran back to his hometown, where he shared the Partideño's secret with everyone.

During the following weeks, the story spread like wildfire across all the villages in Chalatenango, creating great fear among the citizens. Everyone talked about the Partideño's dark pact, and anxiety took hold of the community.

Over the years, many people claim to have seen the Partideño walking barefoot, wearing his enormous hat, and carrying his bow through their lands. When he passes by any livestock that is grazing, be it cows, goats, or chickens, they begin to follow him as if under a spell. He does not need to move a single finger for this to happen.

The owners always try to run and recover their precious animals, while yelling angrily, "The Big Hat Man *(El Sombrerón in Spanish)* stop. Leave my animals alone!" But it is always in vain because no one can stop him! Sooner or later, he vanishes in the middle of the street with their animals, and they never see them again.

A few days later, after The Partideño has stolen enough livestock, he travels to Honduras or Guatemala, where he sells the animals on the black market for a hefty profit. He knows very well that he only steals the crème de la crème.

Nevertheless, since the late 60s, no one has seen the Partideño. Many people swear the police arrested him, and he is serving a severe punishment for all his robberies. Others believe he lost his powers and died. The truth is nobody knows.

Nowadays, there is only one truth among the people from Chalatenango: If you ever see someone walking barefoot with a huge hat and a bow in his right hand in the north, you should be careful because the Partideño might have returned and is going to take all your precious animals!

The Squeaky Wagon

INSPIRED BY VICTORIA DÍAZ DE MARROQUÍN'S VERSION FROM HER BOOK,
LEYENDAS CUENTOS Y ADIVINANZAS DE EL SALVADOR.

What I am going to tell you was shared with me by my foster grandfather when I was a child. The same story was shared with him by an unknown man from San Vicente. That man told my grandfather his grandfather heard it from some old men in a nearby town. This is a very ancient story.

Everything started when there were still many Indians living in the Americas, and the first Spaniards began to arrive at these lands with more and more people on every ship. People lost count of how many came yearly.

Most Spaniards came to El Salvador because their lives in Spain were extremely challenging. There were no jobs, no food, only poverty, and they just wanted to start a new chapter in the so-called New World. This is how Ludovico Díaz came to El Salvador, later renaming himself Dr. Ludovico Díaz de Valdivia.

Ludovico was born in a quaint village nestled in the mountains of Jaén. He was a polite and calm child, and that is why Teodorico de Montijo, a small Dominican priest, decided to educate him, starting by teaching him how to read and write in Spanish properly.

Over the years, the priest noticed the boy's cleverness and decided to teach him everything he knew. He even tried to convince him to become a priest like himself, but the boy never agreed. However, the priest gave him the same advice all the time.

"Look, Ludovico. You have been lucky that you are polite, and I taught you all that I know.

You must always thank our Almighty Father, Jesus, the Holy Spirit, the Virgin Mary, our patron Saint Eufrasio, All Saints, the Pope, your father, and your mother. And do not forget what you have learned because you must use it to help others. Do not forget it!"

"Yes, Mr. Priest," Ludovico always answered.

However, the truth was that he never paid attention to the priest's advice, it went in one ear and out the other.

Twelve years later, the priest Teodorico died. For Ludovico, this meant he could finally do what he had always wanted, relocating to a larger and richer town.

In that town, Ludovico met Mr. Mateo, a priest's acquaintance, who owned a pharmacy. His pharmacy was one of few that could prescribe drugs since he was a recognized Spanish chemist.

Mr. Mateo hired Ludovico because he noticed he might have some useful talents. Also, he could use a second pair of hands since he was getting old.

Ludovico was a curious man, and one of his secret dreams was to know more about the apothecary. He had heard he could become rich with it. Therefore, every time someone was sick or injured and arrived at the pharmacy, he hurried to see what Mr. Mateo was doing. He wanted to increase his knowledge by writing down all steps in detail, and helping his employer because he aspired to become as rich as him one day.

A couple of years later, on his way home from work, Ludovico overheard a plan to sail across the Atlantic the following weekend in search of a better life in the New World. They had heard it was a place full of gold.

"Today is my lucky day!" Ludovico thought. Being clever, he approached them and said, "Excuse me, I overheard that you are going to the New World, right?

You probably have children and wives who may need care if they get sick. I can go with you and support you if you are interested."

"Really? This sounds like a great deal! But we do not have any money to pay you," replied one of the men sadly.

"If you take me with you and give me some food, I will do it for free," Ludovico offered.

The men accepted his proposal, and the next weekend their journey began.

For several months, Ludovico's life was unbearable, and he began to doubt whether this was a good deal after all. So many babies crying, all the time. Too many sick people to attend to and there was almost no food. He met so many illiterate people that he felt dirty and superior at the same time, knowing he was educated and skilled in apothecary. He started to think it would have been a better idea to stay in Spain and wait for Mr. Mateo's death to inherit his pharmacy.

One afternoon, a sailor shouted, "Land in sight!" Ludovico's spirits lifted—they had finally reached land, and he could escape this nightmare. They docked at Trujillo in Honduras. As soon as he could, he traveled to a new city called San Vicente in El Salvador, where he created a new image and introduced himself as a Spanish doctor.

People trusted him because he was a newcomer, and his sophisticated vocabulary captivated everyone he met. Additionally, his knowledge of apothecary and considerable experience taking care of uncountable sick people for many months heightened his message and created confidence among the citizens.

Throughout his life, Ludovico had noticed a peculiar pattern among important people. They always possessed long and eloquent names like "Mr. Rodrigo Díaz de Vivar" or "Mr. Diego

Melo de Portugal." And this was the perfect time to have his own; therefore, he renamed himself, "Dr. Ludovico Díaz de Valdivia."

Ludovico was very lucky without a doubt because, in a matter of weeks, he received a couple of patients who he cured with no effort. Those people started to recommend him, and he started to build a strong good reputation and travel from one town to another, healing numerous people.

However, he was clever and careful because he always told his patients that if they died, it had been God's will, but if they survived, he asked them for a small gift, maybe a small chicken or some silver, but they always had to give him something. That is how Ludovico became a rich and respected member of society.

Things were going better than expected for Ludovico, and one night, he hit the jackpot. He unexpectedly cured an Indian called Yoltic Tecol. He was a healer who was suffering from a severe and unusual fever. Yoltic invited Ludovico to his house, where he revealed many secrets to him about his life and Indian traditions. He offered his friendship and a unique drink as payment for Ludovico's healing. Ludovico pretended to care about what Yoltic was saying, but he was only interested in the sweet, tasty drink. That beverage made his heart really happy.

Ludovico and Yoltic kept meeting each other for several months. Ludovico loved the delicious drink. One day Yoltic said something that caught Ludovico's attention.

"Before the Spaniards arrived, we had many healers like me. However, now, they can only visit us secretly because it is dangerous. The Spaniards believe we practice some kind of witchcraft. Our elders taught us everything they knew. Some of our traditions have been shared orally for over 1000 years."

After those words, Ludovico was thoughtful and did not want to look suspicious. But after a while, he asked, "Look, Yoltic, when you have a little bit of time, take me to your elders. Do you understand? I would like to talk to them personally."

Yoltic was so grateful that he took Ludovico to meet them immediately.

Ludovico appeared trustworthy and humble, so the shamans shared their ancient knowledge with him. He jotted down all instructions and herbs, noting every single detail.

The following weeks Ludovico kept visiting the shamans secretly, enriching his knowledge, but he needed to be careful because no Spaniard could ever discover that he was friendly with the Indians.

After a couple of weeks, he started to test those new medicines. Immediately, people with incurable diseases were cured! He was happier than ever and started to charge a lot of money for a mere drop of water!

He became so busy with his new role as the city's doctor that he forgot about the Indians, including his "friend" Yoltic Tecol.

One day, while Ludovico was talking with some of his Spanish friends at his house, the Indian came looking for him.

"Dr. Ludovico, please come to my house! Izel is in terrible condition, suffering from an unknown illness, and I cannot find anyone to help her. She wallows in pain!" pleaded Yoltic.

"Who is he? What is this dirty Indian doing here?" said Ludovico, pretending he did not know Yoltic. However, one of his friends recognized Yoltic and asked, "Is he not Mr. Cecilio del Valle's servant, the one you cured some time ago?"

"Yes, but I do not know what he is doing around here," replied Ludovico.

"But Dr. Ludovico ... PLEASE, HELP US! IZEL IS DYING!" said Yoltic even more desperately.

"SILENCE! Get out of my house and find one of your own to heal her," Ludovico shouted as he kicked Yoltic out.

After this, Ludovico was afraid that his friends would think that he had something to do with the Indians, and they would discover where his medicines came from. So, he went to speak to one of the most important priests in the capital.

"Your Reverence, please give me your blessing," Ludovico said, "I am a fervent Christian, and I have seen things that may concern you."

"What is your affliction, my son?" the priest asked him.

"Oh, Your Reverence! What I have to tell you is dreadful. I discovered that many or almost all the baptized Indians, and those who are preparing for baptism, visit healers who cheat them with witchcraft. I came across this because my work as a doctor forces me to visit every town that I can," said Ludovico.

"Are you sure about what you are saying, son? This is a serious accusation against healers in our region," the priest said.

"With all the pain of my heart, Your Reverence, I, Ludovico Díaz de Valdivia, swear that is true, and I can tell you who they are because I saw them practicing witchcraft," Ludovico responded, lying through his teeth.

Ludovico accompanied the priest and his delegates to reveal where they lived. He also accused Yoltic Tecol of being one of them.

The priest and his delegates decided that on Saturday afternoon, they were going to imprison and kill all Indians for practicing witchcraft. And as it was said, it was done. One by one, they imprisoned the Indians. The Indians begged for their lives, swearing they would stop, but they were shown no mercy.

By sunset, not a single Indian from that tribe remained alive. One of the delegates gathered Indians from neighboring towns to witness the fate of those deemed disobedient or accused of practicing witchcraft. Three days later, the only satisfied souls were the king vultures, leaving behind nothing but the Indians' bones after their gruesome feast.

Meanwhile, Ludovico walked confidently, certain that his dark secret would remain buried. With the Indians' knowledge at his disposal, he was sure his wealth would only grow. His plan was unfolding better than he had ever imagined.

As for the other Indians, most succumbed to diseases brought by the Spaniards. Ludovico never bothered to check on them.

Years later, a devastating plague swept through, sparing few and leaving countless dead. Ludovico tended only to the wealthy and influential—those who could afford his services. The rest perished and were buried in mass graves.

After the plague passed, the survivors held a solemn Thanksgiving mass in the Church of Our Lady of the Pillar. It was a special sung mass and Ludovico cried heartily, but those were crocodile tears since he never cared for anyone besides himself.

After the mass was over, the survivors went to eat tamales and enjoyed some time together. When Ludovico had finished, he said goodbye to everyone and went to his home in another town.

Ludovico felt incredible—he had grown so wealthy after the plague that he bought a new house. However, before he had left the city, he started to feel as though somebody was following him.

"Oh no! Whoever it is, come out and stand in front of me so I can see you! And tell me what you want!" Ludovico complained angrily.

"It must be some crafty Indian trying to get money from me," he thought as he continued walking. However, after a while, he got the same feeling and stopped abruptly.

"Come on! Oh no! Whoever it is, come out and stand in front of me so I can see you! And tell me what you want!" He complained again in a very unpleasant tone.

However, nothing happened. The night was eerily quiet, with no stars, no moon, and not a soul in sight.

"I would better hurry up," he thought to himself, already a little scared. He only had half a league left to reach his house. He quickened his pace as the house was less than a hundred steps away, but the eerie feeling grew stronger.

"For God's sake! Show yourself and tell me who you are and what you want!" Ludovico shouted, his voice trembling with anger.

No sooner had he shouted than a blinding light fell on him, leaving him stunned. He could not see anything. He only heard a voice that told him, "Aha, Ludovico Díaz, how are you doing? You no longer look like the common people. I can see that life has treated you very well."

"Who dares speak to me like that? You must have mistaken me for someone else. I am Dr. Ludovico Díaz de Valdivia. Everyone around here knows me," Ludovico answered.

"I already know that," the voice said. "The poor and the rich know Ludovico Díaz; the living and the dead also do as I do, because it was me who taught you everything you knew when you were a small kid."

"Oh my God! The priest Teodorico!" screamed Ludovico, terrified.

"Oh, Ludovico, Ludovico! Of all the advice I gave you, one stands out—especially since you refused to become a priest. You promised me you were always going to be a good man, and you were going to help the needy," said the priest sadly.

"But I am a good man! I heal people and am always ready when someone needs me!" Ludovico pleaded.

"Are you sure, Ludovico? What about Yoltic Tecol and the other Indians you condemned to death? And the poor Spaniards who died from the plague—did you help them too? You cannot deceive me! I have seen it all. You had everything needed to be happy and to help others, but your greed consumed you," the priest said.

"Forgive me, priest Teodorico, please forgive me!" Ludovico begged, kneeling on the street.

"No, Ludovico, there are no more excuses. Your time of reckoning has come. You will never know peace again. Follow me!" the priest commanded.

The priest ordered Ludovico to dig a great ditch in a very specific location. After Ludovico had finished, the priest said, "do you see what is there? Those are the bones of all who died because of you! With those bones, you are going to make a wagon. NOW!"

Ludovico began to assemble a wagon with great fear. The priest looked at him carefully and when he finished, the priest said:

> *"Your time has come! From this moment, you no longer belong to this world. Though you do not feel it yet, you are already dead—and peace will never be yours.*
>
> *Your punishment will be to go from the top to the bottom with this wagon picking up the bones of all those who died because of you! You are going to each cemetery all over El Salvador and bury them.*
>
> *Do not think you are alone! There are many wicked souls like you across the land. All of them roam, collecting the bones of those whose lives they ruined, searching for cemeteries to lay them to rest."*

Ludovico lost everything, and because of his eternal punishment, he was never seen again.

To this day, the eerie squeaking of the wagon can be heard throughout El Salvador, especially at midnight, when its unsettling sounds echo in the darkness. Everyone agrees it is a bizarre and terrifying sight—the wagon moves backward without oxen, and as it passes, the ground seems to tremble, accompanied by a chilling, chain-like screech. Yet, the sound is not from chains—it is the bones of the dead clattering inside the wagon.

Everyone knows to stay indoors when they hear the wagon, for the wicked spirits are gathering the bones of those who, like the Indians, died unjustly. Some who dared to venture outside at that hour were never seen again.

A woman from Ataco once told me she heard the wagon near her house on a Friday the 13th. Another man from Santa Tecla recalled hearing it near a school when he was a boy, one Christmas season. No one knows where the wagon will appear next.

It sounds terrifying, does it not? The truth is like the air—you can hear it but never see or touch it. If you dare to learn more, do so at your own risk!

The Owls

Every night, mysterious birds roam the Central American skies: the owls. Their eerie calls echo through the dense forests, blending with the whispers of the wind. They are especially visible during the blue moon when they become more active and fly in unique and hypnotic patterns.

Many believe that these owls are the spirits of witches, trying to scare their future victims. They are said to seek out lone wanderers in desolate places, their unblinking eyes following every step. Be cautious if you walk alone at night, as they may appear before you and transform you into a tiny, helpless mouse. The world suddenly shrinks, your heart races, and the once distant sound of wings now thunders around you. Once transformed, they will hunt and devour you alive!

Furthermore, if you ever hear a low whistle coming from the sky, it is likely an owl flying overhead. The sound is said to carry a strange, hypnotic quality that makes your skin crawl. If you dare to respond with the same whistle, the owl will swoop down and claw at your eyes. Legend tells of a young Indian man who, upon whistling back, felt a sudden rush of wind before the owl struck, leaving him blinded and cursed. Be careful if you ever hear it—sometimes curiosity can cost far more than you expect.

Like all animals, some owl species are more unique than others, and one particularly esteemed species is the bearded owl. Its most distinctive feature is the pair of large, elongated feathers growing beside its beak. When the moonlight catches them, they shimmer faintly, giving the owl an almost spectral appearance. For many, seeing a bearded owl at night is both a blessing and a curse, which is why they are highly respected.

According to the elders, the bearded owls were once powerful sorcerers who were cursed by a shaman and transformed into owls hundreds of years ago. The shaman cursed them for revealing ancient secrets to the Spanish invaders, as he could not allow such knowledge to fall into their hands. The knowledge they possess can either impress or frighten those who discover it.

Interestingly, in some Central American regions, it is believed that to gain the secret of success, wealth, or fame, one must find a bearded owl during the blood moon. The owl must be drinking water at the edge of a lake. You should approach it with respect and offer a piece of the finest meat. If the owl accepts and eats it, it will revert to one of the sorcerers for a few minutes and reveal the hidden secrets as payment. Many have tried, but only a few have succeeded. Perhaps, if you are brave enough, you will be one of them!

The Lady of the Rings

INSPIRED BY BLOG MITOS Y LEYENDAS DEL MUNDO'S VERSION.

During the last years of the Federal Republic of Central America, numerous children disappeared in San Salvador without leaving any trace. This situation alarmed the entire community because nobody understood what was happening. Many Salvadorans attributed these evil acts to a mysterious woman they called the Lady of the Rings.

The woman had an indescribable face and wore white clothes and ten mystical rings. Some of those rings had skulls, while others were impossible to describe. One thing was certain, they possessed unique evil powers.

The woman's actions remained undocumented until one day, a man called Juan de León met the mysterious woman face-to-face. On that terrible day, his life changed forever, ending in a tragic story that is as follows.

Juan was a carpenter in the 4th Western Street in San Salvador. He had a tiring job in the government, providing everything required for the civil war in 1839.

One night after work, he noticed it was unusually hot. Probably over 35°C (95°F). However, he was just tired and wanted to return home, take a shower, and sleep. When he arrived, his wife was reading a new book. She greeted him cheerfully and gave him a sweet kiss on his cheek.

His wife shared with him all the fantastic things about her new book, and they spoke for some minutes. While they were talking, their child asked them if he could play on the windowsill, and they agreed. They thought they lived far from the conflict zone, and their area was pretty safe. Nothing could go wrong.

After the conversation had finished, Juan sat on his rocking chair, and with a heaviness of sleep, he began to nod, when suddenly he looked towards the window and saw the Lady of the Rings next to his child!

Juan could not describe his feelings at that moment because he was trembling like a leaf. He was more frightened than ever before in his life. He had heard that this woman possessed ten magical and hypnotic rings, some with skulls, others with rubies. One was unique and had an unknown power that came from hell!

This could not be happening, he shook himself, rubbed his eyes, and checked again, and there was only his child playing in the window. He thought to himself, "I am just hallucinating from a tiring day at work." He just fell asleep.

After some time, he woke up and saw the lady standing next to his son, smiling at him. At that moment, the lady's rings paralyzed him. He was unable to move or speak, but after several attempts and prayers to the Almighty, he escaped from the lady's powers and ran. He took his child to the room where his wife was.

Juan burst in and told his wife that he had met the Lady of the Rings. The couple could not sleep for several weeks.

A couple of months later, Juan was riding his horse to his work when he saw the same lady not so far from his work. She was standing like a statue with her ten magical and hypnotical rings, but he decided to ignore her and go to his work directly.

At the end of the day, when he left his work, the lady was still standing there. However, this time she was laughing out aloud because she had his child with her. Suddenly, she vanished in front of him.

Juan rode his horse as fast as he could. "Where is our child?" he asked his wife when he arrived home.

"Juan, what is happening to you? Who are you talking about? We do not have any children," she replied.

Just then, Juan heard an evil laugh from the street. He left his house and saw his child with the Lady of the Rings. He tried to catch her, but she vanished in front of him for the last time.

From that day forward, Juan was consumed by confusion and torment. He became insane with guilt, feeling he could have done something to save his child. Furthermore, everyone he knew had forgotten that he ever had a child.

You might wonder why the Lady of the Rings commits such evil deeds. According to local legends, she is a ghost, walking around Central America, chasing irresponsible parents to take their children with her to the afterlife. Therefore, the next time you consider being an irresponsible parent, just remember what happened to Juan because you could be the next one!

The Cuyancua

INSPIRED BY EL SALVADOR MI PAÍS' VERSION.

Long ago, when the Maya people used to live in El Salvador, at the end of a dry season, some Indians discovered an unusual animal near a river, which was massive and was half-pig and half-snake.

The Indians tiptoed and tried to approach it. Suddenly, they heard a dark squawk, and the animal slid into the river, causing it to rain. After this, a new wet season began, and they named it the Cuyancua or the Cuyancuat.

After this first encounter, the Cuyancua became a more prominent part of their lives. It began to appear to announce the wet season or to predict rain, tropical storms or hurricanes, La Niña, floods, among other water phenomena in some unexpected cases.

Nowadays, you can see the Cuyancua in the north of Izalco. Here, the citizens say that as dusk falls, they hear a dark squawk and feel strong tremors beneath their homes, which frightens the local Indian families and the surrounding communities. All these uncommon experiences force them to lock themselves in their houses very early before six o'clock in the evening until the next day when the Cuyancua has left.

It is important to highlight that its squawk is heard mainly in the vicinity of rivers or streams. This creature crawls to find food and usually hides in the irrigation ditches of Izalco, Caluco, Nahulingo, and San Ramón. Those who hear the Cuyancua entrust themselves to God, close their eyes, pray, and hope that nothing is going to happen because most of them know what it meant for the Maya people.

Additionally, those who stay up late and encounter this creature often faint and remain speechless for several days after regaining consciousness. The few who overcame their experience shared it with their relatives and friends. Then they try avoiding the place where they met it. However, this may not work because the Cuyancua does not appear in the same place twice.

If you are brave enough to seek out the Cuyancua, some Izalco residents offer a few useful tips. It frequently hides in the area surrounding Atecozol Spa. Next, it crawls along stream beds, winds up trees, and disappears from human sight for some time. Shortly after this, you can hear it near Nahulingo, where it slides down the rivers to scare the washerwomen of the Río Grande de San Miguel River. In the end, you can hear it in Caluco or San Ramón. Who knows where the Cuyancua will appear next time!

Finally, there is one last tip. If you find pure water springing from the earth where there was not a river before, this is a Cuyancua's sign. Indeed, this new headwater was dug by it, and later, it slept nearby. Therefore, if you walk around it and are fortunate, you might encounter it before it moves on. As an additional fact, this water is extremely pure and fresh, and everyone can enjoy it, so feel free to drink it.

As you can see, the Cuyancua holds a certain dominion over water and rain, which is why it commands respect—something to keep in mind if you ever travel to El Salvador.

The Fair Judge of the Night

INSPIRED BY EL SALVADOR MI PAÍS' VERSION.

Many moons ago, after the Spanish colonization was over, when it was necessary to maintain tranquility at night, an unusual being came from the beyond to bring peace and order.

This being was a ghost, but no one knew what he was until one night, during the dry season of 1821. Some men were returning home drunk and causing a lot of trouble in their neighborhood in La Palma. They did not listen to anyone and continued making noise and mess. However, a strong wind suddenly shook the branches of the trees. It was so strong that the men hit the ground immediately.

When they stood up, they saw a being like nothing they had ever seen in their lives. It was quite tall, perhaps 1.80m, and was headless! They could only see a plume of smoke from his neck. Also, it was dressed entirely in black and rode a black horse. In his right hand, he held a whip.

They shook with fright, not knowing what that being was. However, for a brief moment, the men thought they were brave and began to throw stones, sticks, and all they could find at it.

"Who do you think you are? Why are you spoiling our night?" they yelled.

The men were shocked to find out their stones and sticks did not hit the being or his horse. They just went across through their bodies! The men tried to run, but the ghost chased, whipped, and reprimanded them.

After several minutes, the ghost stopped and yelled:

"RETURN TO YOUR HOMES AND STOP YOUR CRIMINAL ACTS BECAUSE THE NIGHT IS MINE! ONLY MINE!"

And the ghost vanished in front of their eyes.

The men returned to their homes, deeply anxious after their experience. They could not believe they had met a real ghost!

During the following weeks, they shared their mysterious encounter with everyone in their town. Some people believed them, but others thought they were just charlatans wanting to earn some fame. Rumors began to spread—some said the ghost was the spirit of a fallen soldier who had lost his head in an ancient war and now roamed the night, keeping order. In their eyes, only a soldier could be so strict about maintaining peace and order. Perhaps his soul could not rest because his duty was left unfinished.

The ones who tried to refute the story left their houses at night, causing chaos throughout the neighborhood. However, they too encountered the same ghost, which only made the legend grow stronger.

Over the years, the same ghost began appearing in rural areas across El Salvador at night. He emerged as a vigilante of peace and order, punishing criminals and protecting the innocent. Constantly reminding everyone that he alone owns the night, he reassured fair-minded people that they had nothing to fear. Because of his heroic actions, Salvadorans began calling him *the Fair Judge of the Night.*

What everyone agrees upon is that he is a ghost of few words. On rare occasions, when he is unsure about the intentions of would-be criminals, he asks peculiar questions to cross-examine them, gauging their honesty before deciding their fate. If the people are fair, he leaves them alone, but if not, you can guess their destiny.

Indeed, the ghost acts as a judge by his own criteria and delivers justice in his own way. He protects decent and honest inhabitants while preventing disturbances from the lazy and vicious criminals who follow orders from wicked spirits. As a fair judge, he teaches people to respect the rules, and no matter who you are, his punishment is always the same: a harsh lashing with his whip. The people are subject to his rules, which must be obeyed and respected.

The Managuas

INSPIRED BY LEYENDAS DE EL SALVADOR'S VERSION.

One stormy night in the 500s, a powerful lightning bolt struck the Earth. The Pipil chief left his home to see what was happening. He was already worried because this had been one of the most powerful and longest storms of his life. The tribe was losing their cornfields (their main source of food) because of the unstoppable storms. It had been months since the last time anyone had seen the sun.

As the Pipil chief walked around outside his house, he was startled to see, for the first time in his life, a white woman. The woman was magnificent, and it seemed that the storm had brought her down to the Earth. Suddenly, she rose again to the clouds, where she had come from, and disappeared for a while.

In the following weeks, many of the Indians reported seeing a white woman—or perhaps multiple women—appearing throughout the area. The women always manifested at the heart of the storm, right after a lightning bolt struck the Earth. The people became convinced that these women transported themselves through the air, specifically within the clouds. As the storms raged, people began to believe that these beings appeared solely to destroy their cornfields.

After many months of discussing the mysterious beings with neighboring tribes, including the Maya, the people finally gave them a name: The Managuas.

The Managuas became a source of great fear among the people. Rumors about these magnificent, powerful, and terrifying white women spread and grew more exaggerated through word of mouth across Central America. Everyone feared and respected them.

Many people believed that these beings appeared only to worsen the damage in their areas, using their powers to control storms and hurricanes. Some even tried to portray them as old dwarfs with large heads and massive faces, but this version of the story never gained traction.

Only in one region of El Salvador have slightly different stories endured over the years. In Guazapa, the elders say that the Managuas are actually wicked and roguish angels under the orders of the lagoon owners (the goblins). Others disagree, believing that the Managuas themselves are the true owners of the lagoons due to their supernatural powers. The only consistent part of these stories is that they appear at the heart of the storm, destroying cornfields.

Nowadays, some people believe that this legend may have inspired the name of Nicaragua's capital city, Managua. But who can say for sure? Perhaps there is still something left to be uncovered.

Chasca "The virgin of the water"

Long ago, there was a powerful oligarchy living in Barra de Santiago in Ahuachapán. The family man and oligarch called Pachacutec secretly engaged his only daughter, Chasca to Prince Zutuhil to increase his power and wealth.

Chasca was a humble, young, and alluring virgin. She had a magnificent smile, dark skin, an hourglass figure, and long black hair. She was the city star. Every man dreamed of having a romantic date with her, enjoying tasty, fresh fish under the full moon. However, when any man invited her on a date, she politely declined because her heart was already taken.

One night, her father organized a special dinner, where he presented his future son-in-law Prince Zutuhil and announced his daughter's wedding in one year. Chasca was shocked because she did not know or love that man. Her pure heart belonged to a poor young fisherman called Acayetl, who lived on Rook Island *(la Isla Zanate in Spanish)*. He had delivered the tastiest fish during her fifteenth birthday, and it had been love at first sight.

Chasca confronted her father after dinner, but he ignored her complaints. He reminded her how important it was for their family to keep their businesses afloat and how she profited from that. Also, they had to have great relationships with the kingdom if they wanted to expand to other regions.

"This cannot be happening," she whispered to herself. She wanted to escape from this nightmarish arranged marriage. However, if the kingdom and her father gave her no choice, she would fight back in her own way. She would hold onto her love for Acayetl as long as she could.

From that night on, Chasca slipped out of the house every evening. For the following three weeks, she visited Acayetl every night. They sang and danced as if there was no end. Acayetl loved her and cherished every minute they spent together as if it were the last of his life. From time to time, they sailed on Acayetl's boat, where he sang as Chasca danced.

However, one cold night, when the full moon was brighter than ever, Chasca was on her way to visit Acayetl when the unthinkable happened. As she approached the shore, an arrow cut through the air, striking Acayetl in the heart as he stood on his boat, killing him instantly. Chasca froze, her scream caught in her throat, as the world around her shattered.

She could not comprehend what had just happened—her beloved had died right before her eyes. In a fit of despair, she lost her mind. Distraught, she tied a stone to her waist, walked to the nearest cliff, and jumped into the sea, hoping to rejoin her beloved in the afterlife.

The murderer returned to tell Pachacutec, the man who had hired him, the tragic news: his daughter and Acayetl had died. Pachacutec was furious and, in a fit of rage, strangled the murderer with his own hands, killing him on the spot. He had lost everything because of a foolish miscalculation—all his future profits and new expansions to the north were gone.

Twenty years later ...

After Pachacutec's death, Chasca's spirit reappeared at the Barra de Santiago coast during an impressively bright full moon.

That night, Chasca was smiling radiantly and wearing a magnificent dress made of feathers. She and her beloved Acayetl were sailing on a magnificent shiny and white boat. They laughed, sang, and danced with such great happiness that they caught the attention of the people in the surroundings.

People left their homes to see who was laughing so joyfully. They were amazed by that miracle! Their lovely Chasca was back. Chasca and Acayetl greeted everyone and blessed them before they vanished at midnight. The next day those people fished more than ever in their lives.

Nowadays, no fisherman goes fishing during the full moon. They do not want to disturb the virgin of the water and her beloved Acayetl. Thus, Acayetl and Chasca bless their fishing the following day.

The Fleshless Woman

It was 1953 when I was coming back from Chalchuapa to my hometown Santa Ana City. I was driving my new Ford Crestline Sunliner. It was an amazing night, the sky was clear, no noise, no cows in the street, only my car and me. I was coming back from a cool party with my friends. I had only drunk a couple of beers—who cared? I was single and handsome. I was in my late 20s, and everyone described me as the king of the dance floor at every party. My salsa moves were unbeatable, they were from another planet, and a few men had my elegancy and style.

However, on that night, I had a terrifying experience that I will remember for the rest of my life. Almost halfway to Santa Ana, I saw the most beautiful woman I had ever laid eyes upon. She was blonde, tall, white, with blue eyes, and extremely sexy. She seemed like the perfect American girl from a Hollywood movie. I thought it was my lucky night, maybe she would be my Marilyn Monroe, and I would be the envy of my town.

Incredibly, she looked like she was walking in the same direction that I was driving. I could not believe it. I stopped just for a moment and asked, "Hey, what is such a beautiful girl doing walking alone at night? Are you lost? It is quite late and cold, maybe, do you need a lift?"

She smiled and said, "Sure, I am going to Santa Ana City. I never expected that such a handsome man would stop and give me a lift."

I had an adrenaline rush, and I felt like the luckiest man on Earth.

She jumped into my car, and while I was driving, we begin to talk. I was flirting with her, showing off my best skills. She started to giggle and began to seduce me. I can tell you, she was really hot. Her voice was so sweet that I still remember it in my craziest nightmares. It was becoming the most exciting moment in several months. I could not just keep talking, so I stopped my car just a few kilometers from the destination. We began to kiss, touch each other, and one thing led to another.

Nevertheless, several minutes later, I felt like something sharp had hit me on my ribs. When I opened my eyes, I felt like someone had thrown cold water on my face. She did not have any skin. She was fleshless! She was only a skeleton! She giggled one more time and vanished!

For the next weeks, I was speechless. I did not share my experience with anyone because I could not believe I had met the Fleshless Woman *(La Descarnada in Spanish)* and gave her a lift!

Once I recovered, I went to the church and spoke with the local priest about my experience, asking for advice and pardon for my sins.

The priest looked at me solemnly and said, "My dear son, the Fleshless Woman is an old witch's spirit cursed because of her witchery. One day, the police arrested her, and she was shot to death. However, her spirit could not go to the afterlife. She must stay with us until the end of time.

She must scare all men in that street who disrespect women, play with their feelings, hit their families, or are drunk driving. Also, she shows up in multiple shapes, colors, etc. To be forgotten by their previous drivers until they become insane or stop their bad habits."

I was shaking after what I heard from the priest and decided to stop drinking for good. I have not had a sip of alcohol in years. However, a couple of years later, when I was traveling across Latin America, I discovered my story was not unique. This wicked spirit exists in several countries, in multiple shapes as the priest said, for example:

- In Mexico, she is an Aztec legend.
- In Ecuador, people know her as the Covered Lady *(La Dama Tapada in Spanish)*.

Therefore, the next time you are driving alone in the street that connects Santa Ana City and Chalchuapa, or if you are abroad in Ecuador or Mexico, do not stop for any beautiful woman who you think is lost or asking for a lift and if you do it, for God's sake, take care of your life!

The Enchanted Ulupa Lagoon

INSPIRED BY "EL DIARIO DE HOY" FROM JUNE 19TH, 1977.

The Lenca people believed that due to the first eruption of the Chaparrastique Volcano, a huge flying serpent came out of its mouth. On that day, the place was full of magma and ashes, and the flying serpent took refuge in the Ulupa Lagoon, enchanting it. Also, the serpent brought new and unusual animals, which inspired several legends over the generations.

The Ulupa Lagoon, in Lencan, means "place of the eels." It had a circular shape and deep waters. It also had a unique feature: a drainage stream began in this lagoon and led to the right bank of the Río Grande de San Miguel River. The lagoon was about five kilometers north of the Jocotal Lagoon and around two kilometers south of the ancient road that connected the extinct indigenous populations of Xiriualtique and Elenuayquin. It was tiny, filled with pure and crystal-clear waters, and was the scene of the Lenca legend of the "Sa-isis-isis yu-uueue-nana" or "the 400 dancing boys," as this could be translated into English.

Uncountable eels, black iguanas, lizards, crappies, and other uncommon animals lived in the lagoon, but no Indian dared to touch or approach them. The Indians believed these creatures were humans from ancient times. Some sought to prove this belief. To do so, four hundred Lenca boys danced around the lagoon for an entire day, accompanied by an old man playing an ancient musical instrument. When the day ended, they were so exhausted and frustrated by their fruitless effort that, in unanimous agreement, they threw themselves into the lagoon and drowned.

Their action was so insane that they agreed to tie themselves so that nobody could escape. One of them brought a long and strong straw rope from his home, and they tied themselves one by one until everyone was bound. Then the first angry boy jumped, and then the other until there was only one left. He regretted his decision, untied himself, and set himself free. This cowardly deserter was the one who brought the ominous news of the unfortunate fate of the young boys to the people of Xiriualtique and who pretended that all of them had transformed into fish or black iguanas. For this reason, the chief decreed that no one should ever fish or hunt any animal in the lagoon.

The four hundred dancing boys also gave rise to the constellations called Tzurlágua, Astillejos, Pleiades, and the Seven-Goats. These were unique names employed by the Lenca people for generations.

Over the following centuries, the Ulupa Lagoon was endangered by multiple eruptions from the Chaparrastique Volcano. The latest ones known took place in the following order: the first one between September 21st and 23rd, 1787. The second one was on July 18th, 1819. The last one was on July 23rd, 1844, and buried the lagoon once and for all.

An eyewitness confirmed some of these events: the Milanese historian José Antonio Cevallos. He wrote in his first volume of "Recuerdos Salvadoreños" (Ed. 1892) the following: "The lava of 1844, formed its corners by the southwest part of the San Miguel Volcano extending to considerable distances until blinding the Ulupa Lagoon and much of the road that traveled from San Miguel City to Usulután City."

With the enchanted Ulupa Lagoon gone, the legend of the "Sa-isis-isis yu-uueue-nana" also disappeared. Furthermore, several abundant ichthyological specimens, vanished: the black iguana (mer), the lizard (mer-tz'oícon), the guapote (pálul), the catfish (osogé), the pepesca (sháya), the ulumma (orum), the film (cóyum), the eel (úlum), the conga (shíw) and many others.

Our Lady Saint Anne

IN HONOR OF MY GRANDMOTHER OFELIA ZELAYANDIA.

Hundreds of years ago, during the Spanish colonization, a group of eight recently baptized Indians embarked on a special pilgrimage to a town called Sihuatehuacan. These faithful and devoted Catholics were carrying a blessed statue of Saint Anne, which they needed to deliver the following day. The statue was unique, beautiful, heavy, and massive for that time, making their journey extremely slow and challenging—a true sacrifice.

That evening, the sun set earlier than expected, around 5:15 p.m., forcing them to spend the night in an unfamiliar place called Santa Ana (as it is known today), located halfway to their destination.

The next morning, as soon as the sun rose, they drank some coffee, ate tortillas with salt, and prepared to continue their journey. They needed to reach the church on time to deliver and place the statue. However, when they tried to lift the statue off the ground, they failed repeatedly and realized that no human strength could move it. They sought help, but everyone they encountered was equally unable to move the statue. It remained immovable, and they grew desperate.

At noon, an old and eccentric woman appeared seemingly out of nowhere and suggested that they build a chapel at that very spot, claiming it was a divine sign that Saint Anne wanted to remain there. Reluctantly, the group agreed to consider the idea. Several days passed, yet the statue remained unmoved. One of the pilgrims shared the woman's suggestion with a local priest, and eventually, everyone agreed to build the chapel at that place.

Months later, when the beautiful new chapel was finally completed, a miracle occurred. On that very day, the pilgrims were able to lift the statue effortlessly and place it where it remains to this day—the Cathedral of Our Lady Saint Anne in Santa Ana City. From that moment on, the inhabitants referred to the statue as Our Lady Saint Anne *(Nuestra Señora de Santa Ana in Spanish)*.

Over the generations, Our Lady Saint Anne became highly revered for her miracles. One of the most significant occurred during the Revolution of the 44. One of the armies, on the verge of surrendering due to a lack of ammunition and poorly functioning weapons, witnessed a miracle. A soldier saw a beautiful woman—identified as Our Lady Saint Anne—approaching with a bundle in her apron. She offered the soldiers a drink from a pitcher of water she carried, and after that, the tide of the battle turned in their favor.

Today, Our Lady Saint Anne is honored every year during the July Festivities *(Las Fiestas Julias in Spanish)*, celebrated from July 17th to 26th.

The Midnight Yeller

INSPIRED BY THE BLOG "LEYENDAS DE EL SALVADOR" AND THE CREEPY PASTA WIKI: "EL GRITÓN."

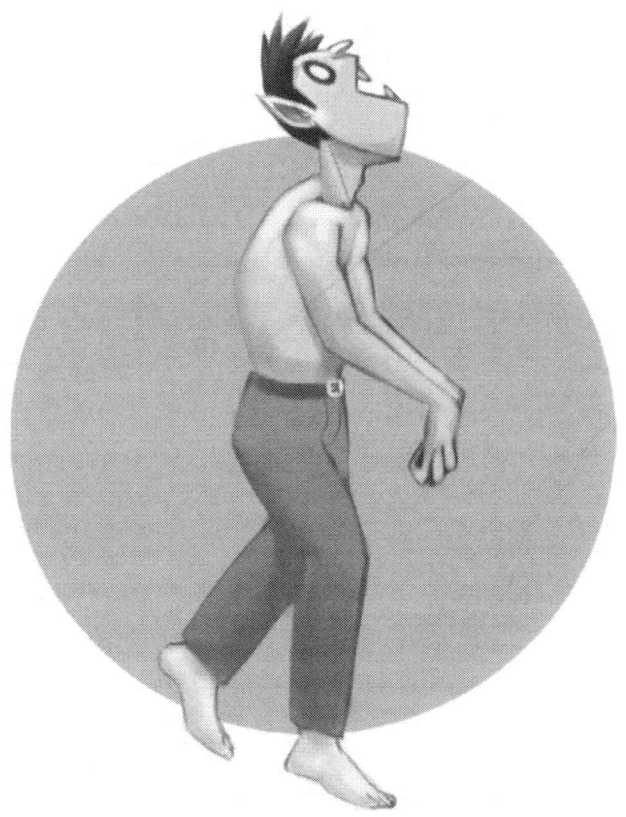

Many years ago, an Indian man was banished from his tribe and forced to live in the forests and mountains of what is now known as Central America. There, a demon took possession of him, and from this fusion was born the Midnight Yeller—a half-human, half-demon beast of enormous size.

In theory, no one can see this creature since it is a spirit, but its eerie yells shatter the nocturnal silence of the jungles and mountains in those lands. However, there is one man who swears to have seen it, his name is Julio, and his story is as follows.

On a Friday in July of 1963, Julio was returning from a wild party in the streets of Santa Ana. He was a very strong man who loved to walk at night. This time, he was walking on a small trail when he passed by El Calvario Church and heard its bell. He thought it had to be midnight and got a little scared and tired. Almost, a block away from the City Hall, for the first time in many years, he noticed that the white Cadejo was not taking care of him. Perhaps, he had been flirting with too many girls and did not remember it because he was a bit drunk. On the corner next to the City Hall, there were about 12 or more dogs.

"Oh!" he thought, "if my Cadejo had been with me tonight, all these dogs would have run away immediately!" On many nights he had strolled alone, and when a kennel of dogs approached him, the presence of his Cadejo scared them away.

That night everything seemed bizarre to him. Julio was too close to the dogs, they stood still. Their ears pricked forward as they looked from one side to the other. "They are scared!" Julio thought. "Poor dogs! They know who their master is!"

Suddenly, it seemed they would attack him. Instinctively, he searched everywhere to pick up a stick or some stones. He had found two and did not have much confidence that he could hit his target with them. Julio knew very well that dogs are very brave animals. Even if he could hit one or two with stones, the others would not stop attacking him. It would have been a different story if he had had a broom. Then at least he could have hit the first one that approaches, then the second or the third, and the rest would scream in pain and escape.

Julio was sure the dogs were acting abnormally. He felt something in the air that night as a warning of great danger. Instead of barking at him, they ran away, terrified, running from one side to the other. A few began to howl as if a demon were attacking them. The howl sounded like they were afraid of death, the plague, or the devil.

At that moment, Julio's hair bristled because the dogs ran away in all directions. He was only sure that something was happening, but he did not know what or where the danger was coming from. He stopped and looked back (which you should never do). Suddenly, he felt a strong warm breeze and saw pigs also running down the street, fleeing from something that he still did not understand.

Immediately after the gust of warm air, he felt a wave of fresh air that violently shook the leaves in the branches of the shrubs of the fences. There was a tremendous yell from behind Julio. Exactly in the street where Julio had been walking just a short time ago, a figure of a man materialized walking in his direction. The figure came closer, growing larger in front of Julio's eyes. With great effort, he tried to move from the middle of the street, but it was useless, his body did not react. Julio was paralyzed and had lost the knowledge of reality.

When the figure reached Julio, he saw that it was enormous—perhaps two meters tall—but it looked more like a shadow. To Julio's shock, the figure walked right through him. Julio had no idea how long he remained rooted to the spot, nor did he remember how or when he made it back home. The next day when he woke up, he was sick with a high fever. He spent three days gravely ill, not knowing where he was or if he was going to live or die.

After a couple of days, his grandfather told him a story.

"You met the Midnight Yeller. You were lucky, my son, if he had been The Black Knight, you would not be telling your story. He would have dragged your body and soul to hell.

Some legends say he is a tormented soul that wanders the streets, scaring some curious night owls to death. If you hear his cry loudly is because he is very far away, if it is heard softly is because he is very close.

The Midnight Yeller is a being that inhabits the most remote towns. It is a large, gray, hairless mass with no head, and it paralyzes anyone who crosses its path. Some brave people have tried to continue their way where he appeared. The first thing they heard was a distant yell that repeated itself, getting closer and closer, until the Yeller stood in the middle of the road closing the way, and then they fainted.

Furthermore, some old men believe there is a technique to protect from his dangerous powers, drawing a cross with a knife. However, when you arrive home, you will be fatigued, and in such terrible shape that you will not be able to move for a couple of days.

In the Trujillo region of Honduras, several countrymen claimed to have heard the heartrending screaming of the Yeller. One of them said, 'I know all the animals of these mountains and have never heard anything like this creepy yell.'

Other people say there are many different kinds of Midnight Yellers all over Latin America. They are spirits of wandering men who died on the paths and in ravines. At night, they yell with despair as if they were alive, while other individuals claim to have seen only their shadows. They say the Yeller is a tall thin man who swiftly crosses the road and then disappears through the bushes. Others imagine or see him as like a tired muleteer, who, sitting on a hill, starts yelling."

Ten years later, Julio was enjoying a few cold beers at a bar near El Tunco Beach when he met a Venezuelan traveler for the first time. The man was journeying across the Americas. They shared multiple stories and adventures, but one frightened Julio the most. The Venezuelan said, "In my country, Venezuela, there is a lost soul similar to the Midnight Yeller who whistles and scares us during the summers. We call it *The Whistler (El Silbón in Spanish)*." But this is a story for another time.

The Lempa River

INSPIRED BY EDGARDO DELGADO'S VERSION.

Long ago in El Salvador, before the gods, as stated in the Popol Vuh, created the Indians from corn in the Americas, there lived a family with supernatural powers. They were the Cuzcatlan demigods.

This family lived in the Salvadoran rainforest where they had full control. They were two elders and two young boys descended from Tlaloc. All seemed great for them, apart from one task which was extremely difficult for them, collecting water.

Despite the fact that they lived in a deep and dense rainforest, they had to walk long stretches through hostile territory to collect it. Worst of all, they had to collect it in clay pots.

The grandfather took on the daily task of fetching water for their chores. He knew the secret of where to find it, but he never revealed its location. Most of the time, his grandchildren accompanied him only up to a certain point. There, he would ask them to wait while he ventured further, returning with two large ollas filled with water. After filling their clay pots, he sent them home with fresh water, never disclosing its source.

They wanted to know the location because, if they did, they could go anytime. They did not need to wait for their grandfather and waste so much time waiting in the rainforest.

One day, exhausted from the hard work of cutting trees and tired of waiting so long, the elder brother decided to uncover the secret of where their grandfather collected the fresh water. He quietly followed his mythical grandfather's trail into the dense, seemingly endless jungle.

Venturing into the jungle seemed utterly insane. There were no rivers, lakes, or lagoons, and the rain was so scarce that the elder brother was afraid to dehydrate sooner than later. However, since he was a demigod, he transformed into a hummingbird and followed the old man through the jungle.

After a few minutes, he found his grandfather, taking a bath in a part of the jungle he had never seen before. It was an excellent opportunity to learn more, and he would not waste it. Drawing closer, he had the greatest surprise in his life when he saw, from the trunk of a gigantic Ceiba, a massive spurt of water. He had uncovered his grandfather's secret.

The young man raced home to inform his brother about his discovery, and they planned how to get the water and stop this painful work once and for all. They planned to cut the Ceiba tree and let the water flow.

The task seemed easy, but they required all the support they could gather. They spoke with all the creatures in the jungle, some agreed to help them, but not all.

The next morning, they gathered next to the gigantic Ceiba and started to cut it. However, by the end of the day, they had made minimal progress and the brothers decided to continue the next day.

The next day, when they returned to the Ceiba and found it intact as if they had done nothing. Not a single cutting mark! The Ceiba was still standing with its water jet undamaged.

The brothers and the animals spent three days trying to cut the Ceiba, but the tree was always back to normal the next day. Everyone thought the tree was magical. However, the brothers were sure there was something fishy here, and the tree was being protected by another being. They suspected it was their grandfather and planned a new strategy to tear down the powerful and imposing Ceiba.

The next day, they arrived with strong determination to tear down the Ceiba. Once again, they focused on the same spot, working tirelessly to bring down the tree. But no matter what they did, the tree kept magically regenerating.

The younger brother left his sibling and the animals working to tear down the Ceiba, convinced that something was wrong. No tree could regenerate on its own. After a while, he found his grandfather casting a powerful spell to protect the tree. Without hesitation, the boy transformed into a scorpion and stung his grandfather's foot with a potent poison.

The old man jumped from pain and stopped protecting the Ceiba for a while. The elder brother and the animals took advantage of that moment and knocked down the Ceiba. When the Ceiba fell, the roar was tremendous. Everyone ran because the great tree caused an earthquake, and the water of the Ceiba began to sprout uncontrollably.

The Ceiba trunk transformed into what we call today, the Lempa River. Its branches became several tributaries for almost 500 kilometers through Guatemala, Honduras, and El Salvador until the Lempa reached the Pacific Ocean. Its leaves and thorns transformed into fish, snakes, lizards, and other aquatic animals.

Devil's Door

INSPIRED BY EL SALVADOR REGIÓN MÁGICA'S VERSION.

In 1824, Mr. Rosendo Renderos moved from Valencia to El Salvador with his daughter Maria de la Paz. He came with many servants and a lot of money to buy fertile lands and start some plantations.

Mr. Rosendo was a widower with a great heart, and his greatest treasure was his daughter, Maria de la Paz. A graceful girl whose unusual beauty impressed the locals, who always said she had the same eyes and the same face as their Virgin of Panchimalco.

For a couple of months, the Renderos family lived in a small house in San Salvador, until Mr. Rosendo found what he was looking for, about 10 kilometers from his house. He bought some beautiful lands surrounded by hills near the Church of Panchimalco. His intention was to plant orange trees with the unique Valencian seeds he had brought with him.

The servants and master set to work, preparing the land to sow the coveted seed. The Spanish servants were insufficient, and they hired Indians from Panchimalco. They constantly exchanged songs and traditions during their work. After a while, the news spread, and they became famous, and the area became known as *The Plains of Renderos (Los Planos de Renderos in Spanish)*.

A couple of years passed, and one afternoon, the local priest set out to enjoy a cup of hot chocolate with Mr. Rosendo and his daughter in their house. When he arrived, the orange trees were covered with fragrant flowers and, very soon, the coveted mature fruit, making a fantastic emerald contrast of the foliage with the gold of the fruits.

Around the town, everyone made all kinds of preparations to celebrate the orange harvest as the Spaniards did with grapes in Spain. They prepared festoons and colored pennants; the priest made a beautiful eulogy from the pulpit, alluding to the festivity.

On the harvest day, Mr. Rosendo, his daughter, his employees, the priest, and their Indian neighbors began to walk excitedly to Panchimalco. The women, dressed in their multi-colored suits with white handkerchiefs on their heads, and Mr. Rosendo and his daughter wore their best clothes. Mr. Rosendo, with his trousers, cinched at his waist with a red silk girdle while covering his head with a wide-brimmed black hat. His daughter with her net dress, her comb, and her silk scarf resembled an authentic Spaniard.

The journey to Panchimalco was extremely challenging because it was a mountainous area. However, no one faced a more challenging journey than the musicians and the Cujtaucujomet Dancers *(performers of a boar dance related to Nahuatl literature)*. The musicians carried their guitarrons, tuns *(percussion instruments)*, and teponaztlis *(slit drums)*. And the dancers wore their special clothes and traditional necklaces of deer jaws. On that day, they would perform a special event to reminisce about the older generations.

When everyone reached Panchimalco, the Spaniards started to sing their Spanish songs that combined the sweetness of Valencia and the sounds of Madrid. It made the audience extremely happy because it was a new experience for most of them. Throughout the day, the blend of Spanish, Indian, and Salvadoran songs and dances made the occasion memorable. Everyone enjoyed the harvest day with pupusas, fresh oranges, several cups of chicha *(an alcoholic beverage)*, and the best hot chocolate in town.

However, at midnight, when the first bell was ringing in the Church of Panchimalco, something unexpected and terrifying happened. A mysterious character whose suit and his horse were as black as night appeared from the top of El Chulo Hill.

From his horse's hooves came red, blue, and greenish flares; the atmosphere became filled with the smell of burning ashes and sulfur. The same demon had come down from the hill.

The Black Knight dismounted his horse, and at the same time the last bell sounded, he saluted Maria de la Paz and vanished with her as if by magic. Everyone felt a strong wind shaking the orange groves and the penetrating smell of burning ashes and sulfur that felt like coming from hell!

Word spread like wildfire that The Black Knight had come down from the hill to attend the orange harvest party and had kidnapped Maria de la Paz. Then it began from mouth to mouth that at nightfall or when the day was darkening, The Black Knight began to haunt the Plains of Renderos.

The rumors reached the Priest of Panchimalco, who was neither slow nor lazy, and he went immediately to visit Mr. Rosendo. They agreed to go on a special procession on Thursday at three o'clock to request the Almighty for his support and compassion.

Several weeks later, no one knew anything until one day, one of the servants was walking near El Chulo Hill when he noticed a strange cabin. He decided to go closer and discovered that Maria de la Paz was there! He rushed back to the town. He spoke with the locals, the servants, the priest, and Mr. Rosendo about his discovery.

All the men devised a plan: they would place a large conacaste trunk at the foot of the window and prepare thick chains to restrain The Black Knight. He would not be able to escape and would be tried for his crimes.

At the first bell of the church, everyone crouched underneath a window to be ready to capture The Black Knight. He was there as if he had been waiting for them and said, "It seems someone found my secret den." All men tried to fight with him, but he was too powerful, and he only laughed because they were like tiny bugs to him. Suddenly, the priest raised his hand and sprinkled holy water over him, but nothing happened. The Black Knight roared, "Did you forget that I am the devil himself? You are just insects to me!"

One of the servants jumped from the roof and stunned The Black Knight for a brief moment. They did everything they could to hold him next to a pole, but it was in vain. He escaped and rode his horse, flames shooting from his helmet, and fled at full speed towards El Chulo Hill. He was getting closer and closer, but suddenly, instead of going up, he crashed into it, splitting the rock in two.

After his collision, he left a gap and fell with his horse into an abyss not so far. Suddenly, there was a strong earthquake and a tremendous storm. The boulders collided, and the orange trees were shaken, causing all their fruits to fall to the ground. Several huge rocks rolled down the hill and buried the entire town of Panchimalco. Many people died, including Maria de la Paz.

The next morning, when the sun had finally dawned and calm had returned, the survivors observed a hole in the hill that they called the "Devil's Door," as they considered it a faithful witness to what had happened that terrible night. Everyone was extremely sad because they had lost everything, and the only thing that remained standing was the Church of Panchimalco's bell tower.

Nowadays, every afternoon along the path that leads from Panchimalco to the Plains of Renderos, Maria de la Paz's spirit walks there while praying for her soul.

When she arrives at the church, she briefly sits on the belfry before disappearing, shedding abundant tears that roll down the slopes. Little by little, the Earth consumes the tears, and joins them at the bottom of a bedrock, forming a waterfall that cascades out from behind the Panchimalco Cemetery.

Some people believe that this waterfall can be found by those with enough faith and a pure heart, serving as a reminder of those stormy times.

Comizahual "The white woman"

One rainy night in the 13th century, a tall white woman appeared from nowhere on the north coast of Honduras. She was roaming alone in the middle of the storm until, by chance, she met the chief of the Lenca people who had left his home to collect some firewood. She approached him and asked if she could stay for one night at his house. He was surprised by her request, and most importantly, by her appearance because he had never met a white woman, but he agreed.

The next morning, the chief interrogated her while they drank cups of sweet corn atole. He wanted to know more as her atypical appearance and unique skills intrigued him. She could not clearly explain where she had come from or how she had reached that place. However, her eloquence when speaking his language, as well as her extensive knowledge of their traditions and rituals. The chief was so impressed that he invited her to stay as long as she wanted in his town. She graciously accepted and began a new life there.

A couple of years later, the white woman had fully integrated into the Lenca society, although the beginning was challenging due to her appearance. However, before too long, she started to travel through the entire Lenca region between the north coast of Honduras and the southeast of El Salvador. There, the people said she was as light as air, flying through their lands in a matter of seconds—one moment in one city, the next in another, helping everyone. That is why they named her Cozumel, which means *The Flying Tiger.*

Cozumel built a unique reputation as a fierce, powerful, and clever woman. She was a natural leader and sorceress who led multiple warriors in several bloody wars. She could cast powerful spells that impressed everyone, even her foes, who were always defeated. She protected the Lenca people from multiple invasions and restored peace, prosperity, and rain during the seven-year drought caused by El Niño. She was a force to be reckoned with.

Over the years, she performed countless miracles, won the trust of innumerable allies, and founded a remarkable empire in Quelepa that endured for generations. Its inhabitants had prosperous and joyful lives envied by all. Furthermore, Cozumel was kind and open-minded, and welcomed anyone who wished to join her empire as if they were the new kings or queens of the land.

For generations, people enjoyed the peace, prosperity, and miracles brought by Cozumel—until one rainy night, she vanished as suddenly as she had appeared. No one ever saw her again.

Many things changed in the following centuries, including the Spanish conquest and the loss of their lands, language, religion, and culture.

Nevertheless, the descendants of the Lenca people never lose hope that one rainy night, their heroine Cozumel will return and bring peace and prosperity once more to their lands.

Izalco Volcano

INSPIRED BY FRANCISCO HERRERA VELADO AND ITALO LÓPEZ VALLECILLOS' VERSION FROM THEIR BOOK, AGUA DE COCO.

Many moons ago, a group of children lived around the Izalco Volcano and enjoyed exploring underground, where their parents said The Black Knight had hidden his treasure.

In those days, there was a large excavation near the cabildo of a church, and the kids discovered the entrance to two masonry tunnels. They were ecstatic and shared the news with everyone. Some people found they could use its soil to make clay. Others thought they were the entrance to hell itself because some people entered and never came back.

After many years, one mayor got tired of this situation and ordered the excavation to be closed and prohibited anyone from entering. Anyone found in the surrounding area had to pay 100 Spanish dollars, and serve 100 days in jail without trial.

Many years passed, and the children grew up. However, one of them, now a man called Fidel, was always curious about that place, and one day he met Julián Uxul, an Indian who spoke Spanish very well.

Julián was a great storyteller who confirmed the story of the treasure and shared an interesting anecdote with him.

"Yes, sir. The Black Knight kept his treasure there. He moved it from another place where it had been buried before," said Julián.

"Where did he keep it?" Fidel queried him impatiently.

"Ah! Don't you know, do you? The treasure was at the factory on the hill in the past." Answered Julián.

"Tell me that story, Julián!" Fidel begged Julián.

And the Indian told this anecdote.

Around the 1700s, there was a greedy couple whose names are unknown because no one mentioned them again after a catastrophe that ended their lives.

They lived on an extensive farm that now occupies part of the volcano and the church. They rented their lands to the poorest Indians, who were their perennial victims. Those lands seemed to be a blessing from God. The corn was three or four times bigger than any you would see today.

However, the landowner and his wife had very bad hearts and insatiable greed. When payment day arrived, the landowners demanded extra rent from the Indians or threatened to take their entire harvest.

Years passed, but the universe never forgets and always takes revenge on those who act with cruelty. Sooner than expected, their cruel actions led to an unexpected twist.

One stormy night, a strange gentleman visited their farm. He wore a black suit, black hat, and patent leather boots. He rode on a superb black horse.

As the gentleman had the appearance of being rich, the landowners received him with extraordinary kindness. Nevertheless, their servants felt an inexplicable fear when they walked next to him. They even noticed all animals displayed signs of terror on that night. The dogs howled with their tails between their legs, and the cattle that were in a rodeo arena began to run towards the mountain with unusual mooing.

The landowners laughed all night. They drank with the gentleman until very late. At dawn, the mysterious gentleman left and promised to return soon.

The gentleman returned every night for several months to finalize their new business.

"What is Julián?" Fidel asked him impatiently.

"The factory on the hill!" answered Julián.

"Ah!" Fidel answered with feigned surprise.

Julian went on to say that the gentleman had told the greedy landowners about a fabulous treasure buried there. Also, he told them he was the legendary Black Knight, but they did not care and celebrated their deal to take out the treasure.

Their business was to make a specific well, and the landowners were in charge of the excavation. They should personally walk to a specific place every day in one of the masonry tunnels inside the volcano. The friend promised he would arrive every night to manage the construction, and he did it.

Three days later, the well had an enormous depth though the digger did nothing but throw the earth in the barrel that hung in the pulley. This was easy! Since it was clear that someone unexpected was supporting them.

Every night, the construction director arrived and picked up his friend. It would have been impossible for him to get out of the well without the help of the powerful partner.

Several weeks later, the landowners were impatient, but the expected moment finally happened. A workman started to yell that he had found something. They could not believe it. The treasure was real and was in front of them. The barrel came out filled with gold and gemstones. In the moonlight, one jewel of multiple colors was covering the barrel with fantastic flashes.

Inside the pit, they could hear the man digging, screaming, "There is more. There is more!" Above, his wife was screaming hysterically: "Is there more? Is there actually more?"

"There is more!" replied The Black Knight, who had arrived at that moment, laughing atrociously. He grabbed the woman's hair and threw her into the well. Then he did the same with her husband and no one ever saw them again.

That same night, The Black Knight took his treasure and hid it in a new underground location.

"And is that all, Julián?" Fidel asked incredulously.

"Wait, here comes the important part, sir," answered Julián.

When the local priest learned of the incident, he went to the farm accompanied by several people, intending to exorcise the accursed place. However, the ritual went terribly wrong.

"No!" Fidel screamed. But Julián continued.

When the holy water the priest had thrown touched the bottom of the well, a terrible thing happened, terrifying screams began to come from it. They were the screams of the condemned.

"Please, God, save us!" Everyone who had followed the priest screamed and started to run for their lives.

For a moment, Julián paused and crossed himself before continuing.

The screams were unstoppable, and while everyone was running, the infernal well began to smoke, and then a column of fire followed it. The Teshcal eruption happened, and many people died on that terrible day.

For us, this is more than a legend. It is proof of what misfortune money can cause and an important reminder to stay humble.

However, do not think only those greedy landowners made this concession, far from it, many more people around El Salvador have agreed on similar terms after them.

And after those final words, Julián vanished in front of Fidel's eyes.

Fidel was in shock and unsure if Julián was real or if he was the spirit of one of those Indians who perished during the Teshcal eruption. He could not believe what he had experienced. He spoke to many townspeople, but none remembered a Julián Uxul. Fidel was so afraid that he never tried to visit the place again. Maybe the saying is true, that curiosity killed the cat.

The Moon's Cave

Long ago, the citizens of Jayaque were humble, living lives centered around work and meditation, free from worry. They understood basic truths, such as the sun hiding behind clouds only to return each morning, its light bringing life and enabling them to farm.

The people gathered around a cave in a half-moon shape and wondered about everything related to nature like the rain, wind, volcanoes, mountains, and everything around them. However, for them, nothing was more magnificent than the moon. It always changed its shape, and during the new moon, the cave was majestically illuminated. They always wondered how it was possible for the cave to be illuminated when the beautiful moon vanished from the sky. Where did it go?

The cave's mystery endured for centuries, unanswered and untouched, until one fateful night when a curious man resolved to chase the beautiful moon, believing that his herculean effort would finally reveal where it went.

After the moon had left the lovely starry sky on that night, the man tirelessly followed its trails, crossing wide valleys and high mountains until he achieved his reward. The moon began to descend, and he was impressed by what he saw because the moonlight was becoming more and more intense until, at the edge of the Shutía River, near a pile of large rocks, he observed the beautiful moon entering the cave that became fully illuminated.

The man was so thrilled that he jumped so high he hit his head on a branch of an avocado tree. He had unraveled the millenary puzzle from his ancestors. He had discovered the reason for the absence of the beautiful moon on those mysterious days. He could not believe his luck, but something else astonished him even more. Little by little, the beautiful moon transformed into a divine and brilliant woman who very slowly and delicately, leaned over the rocks in the form of a half-moon just in front of the cave.

This was unbelievable. He felt like the luckiest person in the world and ran to his town as fast as possible. When he reached his home, he told his family what he had discovered. No one could believe it! How was this possible? In the end, his family trusted him, and by the power of the mouth, the news spread throughout the town. Everyone wanted to see this magnificent woman

From that moment on, during the new moon, all the citizens traveled to the Shutía River to see the beautiful moon transformed into a woman, resting on the rocks of the cave. Everybody sat down, contemplating her without bothering her, and nobody dared to speak with her. They only admired her grace, elegance, and magnificent smile!

As time passed and generations changed, evil became more prevalent in society, filling it with selfishness and cruelty. All this saddened the moon, and she decided to leave and never return to the world of men.

Today, nobody knows where the beautiful moon rests. However, the citizens of Jayaque continue to explore the cave, hoping that one day, their beautiful moon will return to grace them with her presence once more.

The Amate Tree

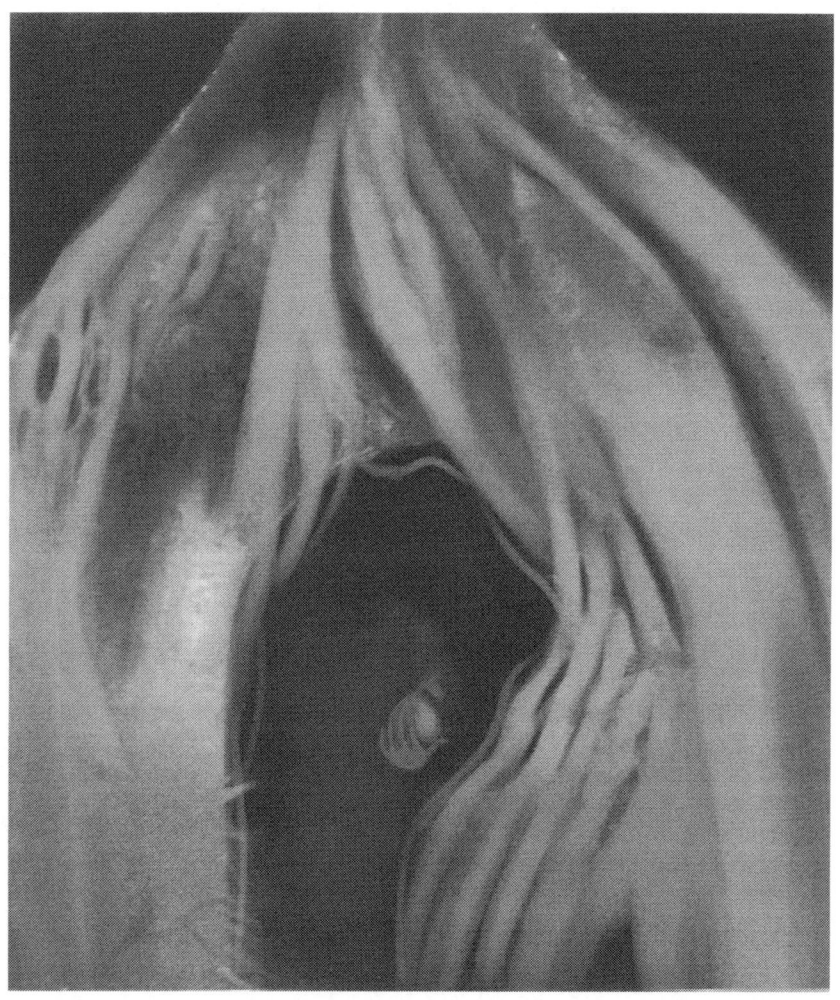

Hundreds of years ago, The Black Knight planted an unusual tree in the warm lands of Central America. The tree spread rapidly across these regions, reaching as far as southern Mexico, and soon became a symbol of fear among the inhabitants. The Salvadorans called it the Amate tree.

People describe these trees in a striking way: their branches are long and pointed, and their trunks are covered with thick foliage. They regard these trees as masterpieces, holding them in high esteem due to their dark past.

In some regions, the elders warn, "You should never sleep at night under them because they throw bones from their branches." Additionally, when their flowers, known as sicono, bloom, only deaf people or children can see them. Children love playing among their unique branches, and more than one has collected their fruits to taste them. The fruit has a beautifully finished, cup-shaped form with a small opening in front, and when it ripens, it becomes fleshy and juicy, resembling a fig.

Many parents have tried to understand this peculiar fruit, believing that agaonidae wasps are involved in its creation.

In Morazán, everyone avoids these trees at night. Locals advise against passing near them after sunset, as this is when the tree reveals its true nature and frightens people the most. Those who linger too long may never return home.

Some brave men have thrown bones at the tree in an attempt to scare it away. However, if they did not do so at the right time, The Black Knight would appear and offer them their most intimate desires. The wise fled, but the weak accepted his offer, and no one knows what became of them.

The Amate tree is truly unique, and if you ever travel to Morazán, you may encounter one shading your path. Be wise—do not linger there!

The Pig Witch

During the 1800s, a woman lived in La Unión. She had an abusive relationship with her husband, who did not respect her. Her husband was an alcoholic who drank at least two bottles of Aguardiente every night. He constantly yelled at her, comparing her unfavorably to her sister, both in beauty and in the bedroom. Her life was miserable, and it did not matter what she did, it was never enough.

Five years later, her husband left her for her sister – who was better at everything. She did not know what to do, in those days divorce was a terrible sign. Her social life was finished, and she was more miserable than ever. She appeared to be an ordinary Indigenous woman, with dark skin, black eyes, and short curly hair. Her age made it difficult for her to start anew.

After many months, she considered committing suicide because she did not have any social life, and her family isolated her too. She became a solitary figure, planning one final trip to the Conchagua Volcano.

That night at the volcano area was colder and darker than usual, and while she was walking, she saw a campfire not so far from the volcano. An elegant man sat by the fire, wearing a black hat and a suit. Next to him, there was an uncommonly big and black horse. The woman tiptoed because she wanted to avoid any kind of eye contact with him, but suddenly he called out, "Hey María! Why are you hiding from me? Where are you going?"

His words froze her blood because he knew her name, but she did not know who he was. She had heard of The Black Knight, but it could not be him, could it? His face was unclear. Curiosity got the better of her, and she moved closer to ask, "How did you notice me? How do you know my name? I do not know you!"

The man chuckled softly. "If I reveal all my tricks, I will ruin the suspense, will I not?" His lips curled into a sly smile. "Come and sit for a while. I think I know what you want."

She felt an unknown force that pulled her to the campfire, and she sat next to him.

"It is good that you accepted my proposal," he remarked, his tone both soothing and unsettling. "I am aware that you were planning to commit suicide in the volcano tonight. However, I have a better idea. Would you not like to take revenge and have the power to do what you want? To remove the person who caused all this misery?"

It was as if he could read her mind. She felt hypnotized by his proposal, though something about it seemed ominous, especially since he knew so much about her. She still did not know anything about him, but fear held her back from questioning his identity. Instead, she whispered, "What should I do then?"

The man's eyes glinted in the firelight. "Not far from here, you can find a small lake. If you swim or paddle with a boat, you will reach a small island. There, you will find a book filled with magical spells. One of them will allow you to transform into any animal at will. Plus, it will grant you other powers beyond your imagination. However, you can only retrieve it during the Blue Moon on January 31st at midnight."

She could not believe what she was hearing. "Why are you helping me?" she managed to ask, her voice trembling.

He simply smiled, his presence already fading. "My work is done," he murmured before vanishing before her eyes, as if he had never been there. She never met him again.

Her curiosity was immense, yet instead of climbing to the top of the volcano, she chose to wait patiently for months. On January 31st at midnight, she paddled to the center of the lake. A spotlight illuminated an unusual book, marked with an unknown symbol on its black cover. She took it and felt an incredible force. When she opened the book, there were some words:

> *"If you read this book, be aware of its power! This is a one-way choice. If you are not sure about this decision, leave it now and stay away from this place. All the spells here are full of black magic, and your soul is not going to be part of you anymore. Be aware of this."*

Fear gripped her, and she became certain that the man had sinister intentions. However, she wanted revenge, and this was the only way. She tried to find the spell about transforming into an animal, and she found a spell called *the pig witch*. The description of the spell was:

> *"This spell allows the witch who invokes it to transform into a powerful and gigantic biped pig with a strong force.*
>
> *After your first transformation, you will be able to transform into other animals like monkeys, birds, chickens, etc.*
>
> *It will depend on your power and experience to invoke the spell. Also, you need ten amate leaves, ten pitos, the fan of a cat, and boil everything for 40 minutes in a cauldron during the full moon.*
>
> *Before you drink the potion, you must say:*
>
> *'Mr. Black, Mr. Black, give me the power to get revenge! Give me the strength of a horse and the wisdom of an owl, but allow me to be unrecognizable to the humans!'"*

She was confused, but she knew what to do. She spent three days traveling to Santa Tecla, gathering the necessary ingredients and preparing the potion. Then, she waited patiently for the next full moon, determined to follow every step.

With nothing else to do in the meantime, she practiced other spells, and soon, rumors of a witch spread throughout Santa Tecla. Strange events began to unfold—people vanished only to reappear weeks later with no memory of where they had been, while others fell ill without explanation. It was terrifying.

Finally, when the full moon of February arrived, she followed all the steps, and this is how the first pig witch was born. She terrorized all the inhabitants of her former town, and her most important targets were her former husband and his new family.

She never allowed her husband to have a normal life again. At every opportunity, she terrified him. She stole from his farm, killed his animals, and destroyed everything around him. One day, he grew tired of the pig witch and decided to find out who she really was. When he discovered her identity, he said, "María, why are you doing this? What happened to you? You were not a bad person. You are a witch!"

She just laughed and scoffed, "Am I a witch? Look at yourself. You are the main reason why I transformed my life and traded my soul for power. You never respected me. You even replaced me with my sister. Nevertheless, I cannot allow you to come back to the city and reveal my secret."

The pig witch conjured a spell that no one knows until today and transformed her former husband into the tree that we know today as the ice cream beans tree. No-one ever knew what happened to him.

She kept terrorizing the city and sharing her knowledge for generations creating more pig witches all around Central America. However, her last trick before she died was to hide the book because, as she said, "No one else shall ever possess this book. It is mine!" Who knows, maybe it would be you who will find it again and cast some new spells from it.

The Tabudo

INSPIRED BY ESA123.COM'S VERSION.

M any years ago, the owner of a magnificent mansion next to Coatepeque Lake went for a sail on a crafted raft near Teopan Island.

The man's trip seemed amazing. It was a sunny and beautiful day, and he could see colorful parrots flying overhead. Nothing could go wrong.

After several hours, the man decided to take a break and fish a tasty tilapia for his dinner. Unfortunately, at that moment, an underwater current dragged him off the raft and into the domain of the Goddess Itzqueyé of the Freshwaters.

The goddess gave him a mission and transformed him into a new and unique being. From that moment on, his life changed forever.

Several months later, he reappeared before his employees, who had been taking care of his mansion the entire time. They had been worried because no one knew what had happened to him or had seen him for months. Some of them even visited neighboring towns, asking if anyone had seen their boss. He had always been a kind and good employer.

However, at that precise moment, their employer was in front of them, and all of them were perplexed because he looked completely different. His legs had lengthened, and his lips had widened, transforming him completely.

The man only smiled, gifted them his mansion and property, thanked them for all their hard work, and said a final goodbye when he vanished in front of their eyes. They never saw him again.

Nowadays, many people agree that his spirit enchants Coatepeque Lake, and they call him the Tabudo.

The locals describe him as a great spirit with a fantastic heart who appears as a small being to all fishermen, but little by little, he becomes bigger. Then he sits in the front of their rafts, and suddenly, they tend to notice something unusual, his legs surpass his head! Most of them are so frightened that they flee as fast as they can!

Nevertheless, the few brave souls who dared to speak with him for a few minutes were blessed by the Tabudo, catching more fish than ever before in their entire lives. Therefore, if you ever travel to this enchanted lake and are lucky to meet him, do not run away from him. Maybe you will get a unique gift on that day.

Mr. Money and Mrs. Fortune

INSPIRED BY MR. PÍO LARA OF CANTÓN BARAHONA'S VERSION, WRITTEN BY VICTORIA DÍAZ DE MARROQUÍN IN HER BOOK, LEYENDAS CUENTOS Y ADIVINANZAS DE EL SALVADOR.

Long ago, Mr. Money lived alone in his gigantic mansion in San Pedro Nonualco, where he had his cattle, coffee trees, and many other goods.

One day, Mr. Money decided it was the right time to propose marriage to Ms. Fortune. He bought the finest gold ring from El Salvador, one with a precious pink diamond. He invited her to a fantastic dinner with pupusas and hot chocolate near Lake Olomega, where she agreed to become his wife.

After their honeymoon, Mr. Money wanted to prove to his wife that he was the most successful among them. He wanted to show her that the pants were more powerful than the skirts, and he proposed a game to his wife.

Mrs. Fortune was intrigued and asked him, "How are we going to know it? Do you have anything in mind, honey?"

"Look, woman, let us take two of my beasts from the barn and ride out to the countryside. I am sure we will find something there," replied Mr. Money.

They rode their horses for a couple of hours until they saw a small cabin in the middle of nowhere. The cabin looked so weak it could collapse even from a gentle breeze.

"I am going to ask for some water there; do you want some?" asked Mrs. Fortune.

"It is fine, let us go," answered Mr. Money.

However, the couple living in the cabin were so poor that they did not have a glass to give them some water. Mrs. Fortune had a flash of inspiration and told Mr. Money, "Honey, let us try here. It is your turn to see if you can make these impoverished people happy."

"Obviously, I can! Who do you think I am?" said Mr. Money.

Mr. Money approached the man in the house. He took a silver coin from his pocket and told him, "Take this and go to acquire whatever you desire to eat. You have more than enough."

Mr. Money and Mrs. Fortune left the cabin.

The man was shocked because he had never touched a coin like that one. He had seen them in the wealthy shops in the city, but never in his own hands. He was extremely happy and took a shortcut to the city. He jumped, sang, and ran down the road. However, after a while, he stopped and noticed that he had lost the coin.

"Dammit!" the man cursed and walked back to his cabin.

A week later, Mr. Money and Mrs. Fortune came back and found them poorer, sadder, and weaker than before.

Mr. Money was puzzled and questioned the man, "What did you do with the coin? You seem poorer than a week ago."

The man replied, "I lost it, and that is why I am poorer and unhappier than before."

Mr. Money had a brilliant idea. "Take these 30 silver coins but keep them safe. Do not lose them again!"

The man could not believe his luck. He took the coins, asked his wife for her old bag, and decided to try once more to get some good food from the nearby city. He told his wife, "This is our day! I am going to bring you all that you want!"

The man set off on foot, but as soon as he entered the city, a gang attacked him. They stole all his money, leaving him battered and bruised. Barely surviving the assault, he limped back to his cabin with a black eye and a nearly broken leg.

His wife asked him, "Sweetie! What happened?"

The man answered her, "Woman! A gang attacked me in the city center and stole everything. I barely escaped!"

A week later, Mr. Money and Mrs. Fortune came back, and the couple in the cabin looked poorer than ever. Mrs. Fortune was laughing out aloud because of what was happening. Mr. Money was blushing as red as a tomato. He was angrier than ever. The man was not able to buy anything, not even a coffee bean!

Mr. Money was so disappointed and angry that he just dug into his suit without thinking. He took a diamond and said, "Take this diamond. You can buy whatever you want, even in the most luxurious shop in San Salvador."

The man said, "Much appreciated." He walked to the most luxurious shop in San Pedro Nonualco.

At the shop, the man started to order the most expensive dresses for his wife, the best suit for him, and all the things that they had never had in their lives. When he was about to pay, the diamond was really dirty and looked like a piece of coal. He tried to polish it up, but nothing worked.

The owner was furious and shouted, "Son of …" He threw the piece of coal to the ground near the doorway. He took his gun and told him, "I want to kill you for all the time that I wasted in a wretched rat like you! You just brought me a piece of coal! If I ever see you in this city, I am going to kill you! Get out of here and never come back!"

The man ran as fast as he could and thought aloud, "another scary experience! The last time the gang almost killed me and this time, this man was really going to kill me!"

When the man arrived home, he was more scared than ever. He told his wife that he almost died this time and would never accept any gift from that odd man if he ever returns.

A week later, Mr. Money and Mrs. Fortune returned to hear more of the poor man's misfortunes. Mrs. Fortune continued laughing as she had before because Mr. Money had failed to achieve anything. Just as Mr. Money was about to act, Mrs. Fortune stopped him and said, "Now, it is my turn."

Mrs. Fortune approached the trembling man and said, "Dear man, please take this cent. At the very least, you will be able to buy a pinch of salt for your tortillas."

The man, feeling a bit afraid, carefully took the cent. He walked slowly along the first shortcut he had taken to the city to buy some salt. As he walked, he noticed a shiny spot on the ground and discovered the first silver coin that Mr. Money had given him.

When the man arrived in the city, the police came with the gang that stole his coins the last time. He was passing nearby when the police called him and asked: "Sir, did anyone steal some silver coins from you a couple of weeks ago?"

The man told them, "Yes, and these are the robbers that stole my silver coins." The policemen gave them back to him and asked, "Do you plan to raise any charges against them?"

The man just answered, "It is enough that you have returned my coins. Take them to your worst room in jail!"

A couple of meters later, two men stopped him again and said: "Sir, our boss wants to speak to you."

The man was surprised and asked them, "Who is your boss?"

"He is the owner of the luxurious shop that you visited the last time." The employees replied.

The man, sweating and shocked, replied, "I will only go if you swear he will not kill me!"

When the man arrived at the shop, the manager said: "Sir! It is great to see you again. Just one day after you left my shop burnt into a fire, I noticed nearby the door where I threw the piece of coal that something was shining, and it was that piece of coal. However, it was not a piece of coal. It was a diamond! I can offer you three farms, 20 cows, and even this shop if you agree to give me this diamond."

The man exclaimed, "Sure, why not? Deal!"

The man did not believe what had happened. It was unbelievable! He was so ecstatic that he came back to his cabin, took his wife, and moved to the city center.

A week later, Mr. Money and Mrs. Fortune returned to the old cabin, only to find it empty. Mr. Money exclaimed, "Woman! You killed them!"

Mrs. Fortune was confident and said: "Let us ride to the city center."

When the couple arrived, Mrs. Fortune saw the man sitting on the balcony of the most luxurious shop there. She asked her husband, "do you know who is that man?"

"No, I do not recognize him, who is? He looks like a newcomer," replied Mr. Money.

Mrs. Fortune answered, "Well, that is the man that you tried to make happy. Now, you can see who really has the power. It is skirts, not pants! Ha!"

The moral of the story is that fortune is more powerful than money, and as Mrs. Fortune always says, "skirts are more powerful than any pair of pants."

Princess Naba and the Balsam Tree

INSPIRED BY VICTORIA DÍAZ DE MARROQUÍN'S VERSION FROM HER BOOK, LEYENDAS CUENTOS Y ADIVINANZAS DE EL SALVADOR.

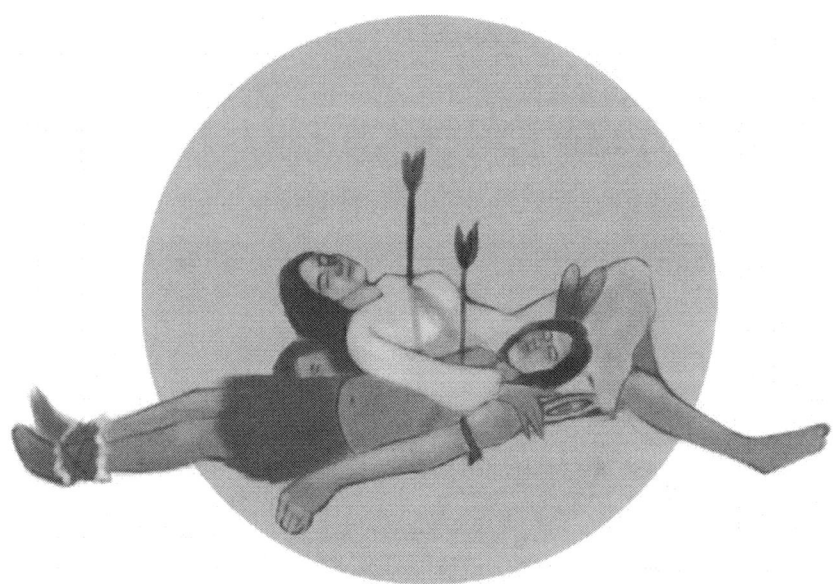

Long ago, there was a terrible war in Cuzcatlan. Hoitzi and the Pipil people fought against King Atlacatl and his warriors. The precise reasons behind the conflict remain unknown, but the consequences were catastrophic and felt for generations.

The war was brutal, leaving countless casualties. One day, the unthinkable happened—Hoitzi died on the battlefield after an archer shot him through the heart.

When Princess Naba discovered that her beloved had been defeated and his body lay lifeless on the battlefield, she secretly ventured out to retrieve it. Naba took advantage of the moment when the king and his warriors were celebrating their triumph over the Pipil people, convinced that this was the beginning of a new empire. To them, nothing could stop their conquest.

Throughout the night, Naba and her six maidens tirelessly tended to the wounded and comforted those awaiting death.

At midnight, some spies informed Atlacatl of what the princess was doing. Enraged and still under the influence of chicha (a strong alcoholic drink made from corn), the king went to confront her.

He demanded answers, furious that his daughter would side with the enemy. Yet when he arrived, he found his daughter lying beside his mortal enemy's lifeless body. In a fit of rage, Atlacatl shot an arrow into Naba's heart, ending her life.

After Naba's death, the king ordered his warriors to execute the other traitors. The maidens were killed with a hundred arrows, leaving no survivors.

The next morning, Atlacatl and his warriors buried the bodies in a pauper's grave, determined to erase any memory of the rebels and traitors.

Twenty years later ...

In the exact place where Atlacatl had buried Naba and her maidens, seven beautiful, strong, and unfamiliar trees had grown. These trees emitted a unique, captivating fragrance, and the Indians discovered that a dark, magical liquid, capable of healing any wound, seeped from them.

The Indians believed that these trees were a gift from Mother Nature, honoring Naba and her maidens for their noble hearts and selfless actions.

Today, Salvadorans know these special trees as Balsam trees—strong and resilient, with the power to heal any wound.

The Tamales Woman of Cuzcachapa Lagoon

INSPIRED BY LEYENDAS DE EL SALVADOR'S VERSION.

The neighbors of Cuzcachapa Lagoon in Chalchuapa say that in ancient times, there was a small cave where the tamale woman would appear at midnight. Later, she embarked on her journey to attempt to sell her magical tamales, saying: "Fish tamales! Tamales! Tamales! Would you enjoy any, sir?"

People who walked nearby said that at night, there was a fire inside the cave. Probably to cook something or to get warm from the cold. However, those who came a little closer could perceive the irresistible smell of tamales.

Some people, overcoming their fear, entered the cave through a back entrance. They always found the tamale woman with her back hunched, cooking something mysterious. However, as soon as she detected their presence, she immediately ran away carrying a heavy pot on her back to sell her tamales.

As soon as the tamale woman left her cave, she yelled in a very sharp tone "fish tamales!" But since the cave had multiple exits, tracking her down was impossible.

In the surroundings, there were always people ready to buy her tamales. They shouted to the tamale woman they wanted some of them. However, she did not "listen" to them and just continued her way through the night with the pot resting on her head. She walked and ignored the shouts of those who called her.

Over time, the stories about the old tamale woman became extremely popular. Many locals and fishermen saw her at midnight, always leaving the same cave, walking among the trees and bushes. Nevertheless, she never wanted to sell a single tamale and she always ignored them.

All those years, no one was able to reach her to buy a single tamale. It was as if the old woman disappeared halfway, and she left the smell of the tasty tamales. She made them extremely hungry.

Some fishermen said, on a certain occasion, a group of daring friends decided to outwit this spirit, trying to do what no one had ever done to buy one tamale.

They fished at night and purposely walked between rocks and the mountain until they reached the entrance of the mysterious cave. Suddenly, they saw fire lighting the cave and decided to go and look for the old woman to buy some tamales.

When they entered, she was there, somewhat plump, of small stature with her back bent, wagging to the pot that contained the tamales. They greeted her politely and asked, "good evening, lady, could you sell us some tamales?"

The old tamale woman kept wagging the pot, without turning them over to see.

"Sit down," she replied, "some are going to come out." And so, they sat on some stones around the cave.

One by one, the old woman began serving the tamales in their garden leaves. They smelled so good that they began to eat them in a hurry. The rich taste of the dough that filled their mouths suddenly changed. One of the men tasted something rotten and shouted, "This meat is spoiled!"

They went to the pot, where the tamales were, and each of them was shocked. Their skin crawled as they saw the contents of the pot: human remains—a skull, a hand, and a foot!

"The tamales were death itself!" they shouted in fright and fled.

At that moment, the old tamale woman let out a dark scream that echoed throughout the lagoon, haha haha! Now you know, my tamales' secret ingredients! Haha haha!

Many people, who were around the cave, saw her pale and disfigured face with a twisted smile that caused terrible fear. Nobody knows if this old woman was a ghost or a witch. However, one thing was for sure, the craziness in her eyes was uncanny.

To this day, on some nights, those who walk near the lagoon's entrance can still hear her eerie scream. Those who frequent the lagoon can still see the fire inside the cave and smell tasty tamales. Nevertheless, nobody dares to want to confirm the story. What about you? Do you want fish tamales?

The Living Rock of Nahuizalco

Long ago, during the Spanish conquest, a Lord of Burgos tried to force Prince Atonal's daughter, Atlakaki, to become his slave.

Atlakaki was the most beautiful woman in her town. She had always attracted much attention, but she was powerful, and her determination to accomplish anything was more than any man, including her father, could handle. She truly honored her name, which meant *the Indomitable Woman.*

The lord tried everything to subdue her, but nothing worked. She would never allow a foreign invader to have any control over her.

One night, after several weeks of torture and forced labor, she yelled at him that she would never become either his slave or his wife, but if he ceased his cruelty and spared her life, she would prepare a delicious and unique meal for him. The lord suspected there was something deceitful in her proposal, but he accepted.

The following Friday, Atlakaki spent several hours preparing the special meal for him and his guests. The meal was unlike anything he had ever seen, full of unique fruits, pastries, and a particular yellow beverage that she called atole. The lord wanted to make a toast to honor his guests, but first, he called a slave, opened his mouth, and gave him a cup of the atole.

The slave had barely finished the drink before collapsing to the floor, foam pouring from his mouth. The boy died in front of everyone. The lord uncovered the princess' trick and discovered that she had mixed coral snake venom into the drink to kill him.

Atlakaki was imprisoned and subjected to a hundred lashes. After the terrible punishment, the princess neither bent nor died. She was truly indomitable. The lord grew weary of this woman and decided to fasten her with tule vines and bury her alive.

The next morning, a servant dug a massive hole, and she was thrown inside. Over the ditch, they placed an enormous rock so that she could not possibly escape. However, she had the strength to proclaim that she would live eternally within the rock, and from that day on, the rock has been moving around the city as a reminder of her massive will and power.

Nowadays, Salvadorans say the Living Rock has its own will and moves from one place to another. It has been seen in multiple places, but mainly in Juayúa, where its favorite spot is La Guacamaya Corner.

However, many people swear they have seen the Living Rock on Techical Street. The word Techical means "sacred song." If you are one of the lucky ones to encounter the rock on Techical Street, you can discover a natural corridor with some ancient stairs not far from it. It is in a kind of balcony-shaped cave, and if you are brave enough to go down, you will experience a unique journey to ancient times.

Alegria Lagoon Siren

Many moons ago, around the 12th century, a Lenca girl lived in a village called Guaymitique, which means "the place where the winds whistle." The girl's name was Xiri, which means star.

Xiri lived with her parents, brothers, and other relatives in a small wooden cabin. Their life was good because their tribe was very hard-working, humble, and smart. Most of them were farmers. They always avoided any potential conflict with their neighbors, until the Tecolucas-Nonualcos attacked.

The Tecolucas-Nonualcos had come to conquer, seize their lands, kidnap and rape their women, and steal all their gold. Their leader was Lamani, the most powerful shaman of those times. He was ruthless, cruel, and wanted to have full control of the entire region.

Lamani and his warriors conquered and destroyed everything in their path extremely fast. No one could stop them. However, when Lamani reached Xiri's cabin, he fell in love with what he had seen. He decided to kidnap Xiri and make her into his trophy wife.

Lamani had saved Xiri from the war and destruction. Nevertheless, Xiri's family was unlucky. They immediately perished after some archers attacked the open market where they were selling fruits on that unfortunate day.

When the gods discovered that bloody war, they forced the Tecapa Volcano to erupt with great fury because they had had enough.

The eruptions continued for several months, and they became stronger every time they happened. Many thought it was the end of the world.

Over the following months, after Xiri's tribe had lost, Lamani tried to gain her affection. However, she always rejected him and would never accept his love. She had lost everything in that terrible war.

One day, exhausted by Xiri's continued rejection, Lamani resorted to his final trick. He pretended he could read the future. He killed a stray dog, took out its entrails, and pretended to read them, claiming that a human sacrifice was necessary to calm the volcano's fury. Specifically, it had to be a beautiful woman, or Xiri had to become his wife.

Xiri did not believe him and rejected his proposal. Therefore, she was chosen as the sacrifice to stop the volcano's fury, whose lava flow and eruptions threatened to devastate the rest of the region.

Lamani called his warriors, and they escorted Xiri to the top of the volcano, where she was to be sacrificed in the lava river. However, at that specific moment, a turquoise-browed motmot appeared from nowhere and began to sing. Its song was so deep, melancholic, and convincing that the volcano began to calm down suddenly. Lava stopped flowing and the volcano stopped expelling rocks and smoke.

Suddenly, the bird song became so copious that instead of flowing lava, strange sulfurous water began to fill the volcano crater extremely fast, transforming it into the Alegria Lagoon. The witnesses believed that the sulfurous waters were the volcano's tears.

Once the strange water had filled the volcano crater, the skies cleared, and some gods appeared. They transformed Xiri into a graceful siren who would live in the lagoon forever. Afterwards, they punished Lamani and his warriors for their war crimes, banishing them to hell, where they would pay for their sins perpetually.

Over the following centuries, the locals have attributed many youngsters' disappearances to the siren. They always warn you, "You should never swim in the Alegria Lagoon because that's what those foolish youngsters did. The siren attracted and kidnapped them using her melodic voice. No one saw them again. Beware."

"If you want to see changes in our world, become an agent of change by taking the first step." Mr. π

Printed in Great Britain
by Amazon

9aab847f-eb87-4f17-b02e-26acb3e56a72R02